TAKE ME SLOWLY PART 2

AURORA HOLLOW DUET
BOOK TWO

MAGGIE ALABASTER

1

———

LEAH

THOUGHTS TUMBLED THROUGH MY BRAIN, fighting to be heard. None of them made any sense. A smattering of images might have been memories. Unless I imagined them.

Maybe none of it was true and I was losing my mind.

It *couldn't* be true.

Breathe in.

Breathe out.

Try to slow my panicked, racing heart.

Think.

Logically, what could be true?

What was real? I forced my mind back to the present. Right here, right now. That was real.

A cold breeze wound around me and ruffled my

hair. The ground was hard under my knees. A sharp piece of gravel dug into my right kneecap. The air was heavy with the smell of trees and fallen leaves.

The creek…

The creek wandered past a couple of small cottages before disappearing into the thick of the forest. The creek they said Coral Clarke fell into. She fell in and was never seen again. That was what they believed for twenty years. That had to be the truth. Right? My imagination had to be filling in the blanks. Making me think things that weren't true.

I lowered my hands from my face.

Josiah Lachance looked at me, his hands raised in front of him like he wasn't sure if he should try to touch me or not.

"What the fuck are you doing here?" He took a step closer, gravel crunching under his worn black boots.

My brow creased. What *was* I doing here? I struggled to remember as I climbed back to my feet.

"Nails," I said finally. "You left a bag of nails in town. I drove up here to give them to you." I don't know why that seemed important. At the time it had. Now? It seemed inconsequential.

"I would have gone and got them." He crossed his

arms over his muscular chest, his defensive walls right back up in place. "You didn't need to bother."

I ignored him and looked around. "You live here? Is it just you?" I hadn't seen anyone else since I arrived. No one appeared from the cottages to ask what was going on.

The muscles in his jaw tightened. "I told you not to give a shit about me. I'm not worth it."

"I get to decide that," I said, barely glancing at him. I nodded toward one of the cottages. "You live there. Gavin Clarke lived in that one with his daughter." I gestured towards the house closer to the creek.

Josiah's eye twitched. "That's right. So what?"

"Does anyone live there now?" I started toward the Clarke house.

"What the fuck?" Footsteps muffled by the grass underfoot, he caught up to me. "You shouldn't be here."

"Shouldn't I?" I glanced over at him. "If no one lives there, then why do you care?"

"I'm the caretaker here," he said. "It's my job to give a shit."

"Why did Gavin Clarke live here?" The closer I got to the cottage, the harder it was to breathe.

"Fuck." Josiah ran a hand over his dark hair.

"Because he was the caretaker. He and my dad used to run the resort. My mother was the cook."

A memory popped into my head, of a summer evening spent grilling, eating and laughing beside the creek.

Imagination, I told myself. It had to be.

"What happened to your parents?" I asked gently.

"They retired a couple of years ago." He frowned, his eyes fixed on me. "You have a lot of questions, city girl."

Yes, I did, and they were increasing by the minute.

"Are you some sort of undercover journalist? Is that why you're here? Those nails were a convenient excuse to come up here and stick your nose in where it doesn't belong?"

"Definitely not," I scoffed. "I don't know why I needed to come up here, I just did."

"What the fuck happened?" We reached the Clarke cottage and he stepped around me to lean against the wall beside the door. As if he was on guard against me trying to break in.

He lifted his chin and looked down at me, his eyes narrowed. "When you got out of your car, you looked like you saw a ghost. Or are you that eager to get on your knees for me?" His cheek twitched slightly, like a smile threatened before he shoved it back.

My lips parted. I wanted to explain what happened, but I didn't know myself. I was certain I'd been here before, but the more I thought about it, the less it seemed possible. I might have seen the place on TV or in a movie. Read about it in a book. Maybe someone painted it and I saw their work. It was beautiful up here, and quiet. The wind like a whisper, like it didn't want to disturb the tranquility.

Coral Clarke was dead.

I couldn't be her. Could I?

"I don't know," I said finally, aware of his scrutiny. "You wouldn't believe me if I told you."

From the expression on his face, we could agree on that.

"You should get back in your car and go back to Aurora Hollow, before you do something you'll regret." His eyes were dark and certain. Convinced I should walk away while I could. Sure I should run and never look back.

"Can I look inside?" I nodded toward the cottage.

Just when I thought he couldn't get more rigid, his entire body stiffened. "Why would you want to do that?"

I couldn't explain why; I needed to. If only to assure myself I'd never stepped foot in there before.

"No one lives there," I said easily. "The lease on the cottage I'm renting will be up soon. I might need somewhere else to live." It was as good an excuse as any, but predictably, he didn't buy a word.

"You're not living up here," he said. "For one thing, your boyfriends wouldn't allow it."

"They don't get to decide where I live," I said tersely. But he was right. Connor and Riley would lose their shit if I lived near Josiah. So would the rest of Aurora Hollow.

They welcomed me, but how welcoming would they be if I lived up here?

"This place would make a perfect art gallery," I said lamely. That was a more plausible story. It was quieter up here than it was in town. This would be a perfect place to paint and create. The cottage looked big enough to host retreats for other artists. I could picture them already, glass of wine in one hand, paintbrush in the other, sharing methods and tales in the shade of the trees.

"You can't rent it anyway," Josiah said, bursting my pretty bubble. "Gavin Clarke owns the place and he hasn't rented it out since Coral left." A haunted look passed through his eyes before he forced his cold mask back into place.

"Has anyone else been inside?" I asked. My eyes lingered on him for a moment before I peered in through the window beside the door. The curtains were open, giving a view of the living room. "You have, haven't you? You look after this place as well. You must have a key."

His lips tightened, but he shrugged. "Someone has to keep the place from falling down."

There was more to it, but I decided not to push yet.

"This is going to sound weird, but I feel like I've been here before," I said softly. "This place. This house. It's... I don't know. Familiar."

"Don't," he said firmly. "Don't start making up bullshit because you're nosy. What is it with city folk, anyway? Always thinking they can poke their noses in other people's business. How about you go find someone else to piss off? I have better things to do." He pushed past me and stomped away.

"Coral's bedroom was purple," I blurted out. "Light purple, with dark purple curtains. And... Unicorns. There were unicorns."

He stopped a few metres from me, his back turned. "How do you know that?" Without looking around, he shook his head. "You're guessing. Tons of little girls like purple and unicorns."

"She had a rainbow-coloured teddy bear with a pink and purple dress," I said, the words coming to me without me thinking. "She had a star on her chest, in glitter or sequins. Like a pop star. She used to think her bear would have concerts when she wasn't there. Sometimes, she'd line up her toys and put on her own concert."

I blinked a couple of times, trying to understand where all of that came from.

Josiah turned around slowly. "Isn't that something all kids do?" But his face was a shade or two paler.

I wasn't sure how to answer that. "My mother said plush toys were a waste of time. That I should forget about them." I'd cried myself to sleep in a room full of practical things. Books I loved, but the room lacked warmth until I placed some of my own art around the space.

"Coral had so many of them you had to push them aside to sit anywhere," Josiah said absently. "Her favourite one was Ms—"

"Ms Sparkles," we both finished together.

He gaped at me. "Who the hell are you?"

I shook my head slowly. "I don't know. I thought I knew, but now…"

"You must have come here as a kid," he said. He paused and his tone changed, became colder. "You've come up here before. What did you do, break in? That's how you know what her room looks like." He took a step toward me, his expression menacing.

I managed to stand my ground. He was intimidating, but I wasn't scared of him. Underneath all of that bravado, he was a man ostracised by his entire community. Ten years my senior, but somehow still little more than a scared boy. One who needed someone to listen, although no doubt he'd deny that.

"I haven't been up here since I arrived in town. I sure as hell didn't break in anywhere." I glanced back toward the living room. It was too dark inside to make out much. "Is the place the same as it was when she left?"

"Gavin didn't touch it," Josiah said after a few moments hesitation. "I haven't either."

"Coral's mother?" I ventured. I remembered someone saying she'd left around the same time Coral did, but I didn't know anything more than that.

"Has nothing to do with the place," Josiah said. "I never saw her after Coral left." He scrubbed a hand over his jaw. "Or before. I don't know, it was a long time ago."

Yes, it was. He lived with the shadow of this for twenty years. Beating himself up about it on a daily basis. I only had to look around at how well looked after everything was to know he'd put everything of himself into this place. He maintained it, kept the place from falling apart. As if somehow that would assuage some of the guilt he still felt. As if somehow it would stop him from being eaten alive by the past.

"Can I please have a look inside?" I asked softly. "Maybe I'm imagining everything. Projecting the childhood I wish I had." There were worse places to grow up than a tight-knit community like Aurora Hollow. "Ms Sparkle has to be a common name for a teddy bear, right?" If I googled, I'd probably find they were a hot trend twenty years ago. Millions of kids all over the country could have had one.

Yet, I knew that wasn't the case. Whatever the teddy bear trend was twenty years ago, it wasn't for bears named Ms Sparkle.

Josiah sighed. "If I don't let you in, you're going to break in, aren't you?"

"Absolutely," I agreed. Breaking in wasn't on my agenda until he mentioned it, but I needed to see inside. Whatever that took, I'd do it. Even if it meant breaking the law.

"Don't make me regret this." He shoved his hand into his pocket and pulled out a set of keys. Stepping past me, he slid one into the lock and pushed the door open. He was close enough to smell leather and pine. Earthy and honest. Heat radiated off him, along with a healthy dose of second thought. Wondering if he should herd me back to my car and away from here.

But I was here now and I wasn't going to change my mind. Wasn't going to back down. More than anything else, I needed to see inside this cottage. If only to reassure myself I had a healthy imagination.

I half-expected the door to creak, but it didn't. It opened without any effort at all, sliding over worn hardwood floors and letting in more of the light from outside.

I sucked in a breath, moved past him and into the house.

2

***

LEAH

I ADDED 'house doesn't smell musty' to the short list of things I half-expected but was wrong about. I should have known, from the state of the outside of the house, that the inside would be well-maintained.

There weren't any personal items in the living room. Nothing to indicate the personalities of those who used to live here. The couch under the window was positioned precisely, as were a pair of armchairs. All of them sat within reach of mismatched tables, one coffee table and two side tables.

The place was cozy. Familiar, but not pinging direct memories in my brain. Not really. Just… Something about gingerbread. And a Christmas tree in the corner beside the wood stove, but that was all.

I could have seen that in a photo. After all, it was the best place for it, as if the layout was designed for just that purpose. If Santa had a cottage, it might look like this.

I moved past the small kitchen that smelled like lemon, and into the room at the back of the house. The room, I couldn't help noticing, that was in almost the same position as my bedroom in my rental. At the rear of the building, with the best view of nature outside the window.

"This one was—" Josiah started.

"Coral's room," I finished before he could.

The lavender walls were almost obscured by shelves full of plush toys and books. A purple plastic chain hung from the ceiling beside the bed, with more plush animals dangling from clips the entire length to the floor. Curtains that draped to either side of the window were darker purple and covered in unicorns.

I took in all of that in a moment before my gaze dropped to the bed. The covers were purple and blue, with accents in pink and yellow. Right in the middle lay a teddy bear. A rainbow teddy bear.

My breath caught in the back of my throat. "Ms Sparkle." I reached out a hand, but Josiah caught my wrist before I could touch the plush bear.

"Don't. You've seen what you came to see, it's time you left." His fingers were almost tight enough to bruise my skin.

"Gavin didn't change anything," I whispered. "It's been exactly like this since the day Coral..."

"Died," Josiah said bluntly. "You can say it. Everyone else does."

"Except you." I pulled my hand back until he let go of my wrist. "You don't believe she died."

He was silent for a moment before he said, "It doesn't matter what I believe. It's not going to bring her back."

"That's why you took care of everything," I said. "Because you don't believe that either. You did this because you're sure she'll come back some day. You wanted all of this ready for her."

He averted his gaze, but scoffed. "That's fucking ridiculous. This is a kid's room. It should have been cleaned out years ago. I'll get some boxes. Throw all of this in the trash. Gavin doesn't want it." He stepped toward the door as though he was about to do just that. Toss everything in boxes and throw it away. Finally put Coral's memory to rest.

"If it was so important, you would have done it a long time ago," I said. "I don't believe it. You think she's still alive and she's going to come back for her things. Because seeing them the way they were might help her cope with whatever happened."

That or this was a sad shrine to a dead kid.

"You're a therapist now?" he snapped. "Don't feel sorry for me and don't analyse me."

"What happened that day?" I trailed my finger down the chain of plush animals, stopping to stroke the fur of a white plush cat. Here and there were patches of other colours. Paint, as far as I could tell. The cat must have sat beside Coral while she did some artwork. Or maybe the paint was on there on purpose, as her own kind of decoration. There did seem to be a pattern to the appearance. A series of small dots across and down its back.

He bristled. "Why do you give a shit?"

I looked over to him, into his brown eyes. "Because someone has to. They said you believe someone took her." Connor and Riley told me he'd claimed he ran after them, but couldn't keep up. That he'd been telling that story for twenty years, and no one would listen.

Josiah closed his eyes and ran a hand over the back of his neck. "Yeah. She was playing outside and I was raking leaves. Keeping an eye on her." That seemed important to him. Like he wanted me to make a note of that particular detail.

I nodded that I understood and gestured for him to continue.

His eyes glazed as he thought back. "A car pulled up. A man, maybe two. They grabbed her, put her in the back of the car and...drove away. It was so fucking quick. I ran after them, shouted at them to stop. They didn't fucking stop." He cleared his throat and shrugged. "That was it."

"Then what happened?" I asked. "You must have told someone." Imagining what kid-Josiah saw made my heart hurt. Seeing something like that and being unable to stop it must have been a special kind of hell. A thing like that would haunt a person for the rest of their lives.

And Coral? I felt her fear as she was grabbed from her home, locked away in a vehicle and stolen. She must have cried. Must have curled up on the seat, wanting nothing more than to be taken back to her father. To her life.

"I told my dad." Josiah's hands curled into fists at his sides. "He told me to stay out of it and not say anything. They'd sort it out. Next thing I knew, everyone was saying she fell into the creek and drowned. I kept trying to tell them that was not what happened. But they decided, and hell if they'd change their minds."

If his jaw was any stiffer, it might shatter. His fury was barely contained, even after all these years. It would have hurt like hell, insisting he saw what he saw, only to be dismissed.

"Did your father believe you?" I asked.

"My father wouldn't talk about it," he said slowly. "Every time I tried to bring it up, he got mad."

"So you stopped bringing it up," I said. That was understandable. Kids could be resilient, but a person could only take being shot down so many times before they stopped putting themselves out there. Especially when it was your own parent who didn't want to know.

Josiah sat down on the end of the bed. He picked up the rainbow bear and straightened the front of her little dress. The gesture was touching, almost sweet, especially given he was dressed from head to toe in black. The rainbow teddy bear was a stark contrast to the badass image he tried to convey.

"Yeah, I stopped. No one believed a word I said. Fucking no one." He didn't bother to try to hide his bitterness.

I sat down beside him. "I believe you."

He snorted softly. "Why would you? Maybe I'm making it all up. Has it crossed your mind I might have thrown her into the creek? You know what they say about us loners. We're probably serial killers or some shit. For all you know, I murdered my parents and you're next." He raised his stubbled chin, as if daring me to deny the suggestion.

"You're not going to murder me," I said. "Believe it or not, sitting there with a rainbow teddy bear in your lap says to me you're not as unhinged as you want me to think."

"I might be *more* unhinged." He glanced over at me and hesitated before offering me the teddy bear. "Ring any bells?"

His expression was tentative, like he wasn't sure if he should even let me touch the bear, much less hold her. Like somehow the plush animal was a sacred object that shouldn't be defiled by a mere mortal like me. But there was more to it than that. He hadn't had anyone to share any of this with for far too long. He wasn't sure if he could trust me, but he needed someone to confide in. To finally have someone understand what he'd been going through all this time. To really listen instead of yelling at him to go away.

In some ways, this was important to both of us. Even if the truth was painful, he needed to be talked about. To finally be aired and put to rest.

I took the bear and ran a hand over the top of her

head and her soft ears. Brought her to my nose and inhaled the faded rose scent that lingered on her. Something about that scent smelled like home. Like a comfortable place I hadn't been in so long. Somewhere I was loved and cherished. Not ignored and treated like a burden, or the clichéd redheaded stepchild. I wasn't even a redhead.

"When I first got up here, I thought…" I wasn't sure if I could put my thoughts into coherent words.

"You thought you'd get down on your knees and suck me off?" he said lightly.

I elbowed him. "I'm sorry to say that wasn't what crossed my mind."

"There's still time." He cocked his head at me. "Okay, I shouldn't ask, but what did you think?"

"You'll think I'm losing my mind," I said. "You'll probably ring up…whoever it is that takes away crazy people around here." I flapped a hand vaguely towards the door. As if a flood of people was going to come and drag me away for my own safety and that of the rest of the world.

"If there was such a person, they would have taken me away a long time ago," he said with a smirk. "Serial killer, remember?"

"You're not a serial killer," I told him. A loner, yes, but not a murderer. I was safe here with him. For some reason I couldn't put my finger on, I trusted Josiah Lachance. It wasn't only because pretty much everyone in town told me to stay away from him. I was drawn to him the same way as I was drawn to Aurora Hollow. He had secrets I want to uncover.

Secrets I might be a part of.

I took a long, slow breath, inhaling more of the scent of Ms Sparkle. Something about her made me feel brave. Like one small teddy bear could comfort me enough to get through the next few minutes.

Finally I said, "I believe what you said about Coral. That someone took her." I let the words sink into his mind and into my own. Allowing the implications to become thoughts. "That means there's a chance she's still alive."

"Depending on what they wanted with her," he said, his voice a low whisper. "They might have..." He swallowed hard, like he was trying to stop himself from being sick. That thought must have crossed his mind too many times in the last twenty years. In some ways, thinking she was dead might have been more merciful.

"Right," I said quickly. "They might have. But the possibility is there. What if she is alive? What if she returned to Aurora Hollow because the place was calling to her?"

He squinted at me. Froze with his expression like that. "What are you saying?"

"When I first got up here and got out of my car, it hit me," I whispered. "I've been here before. Because I used to live here. My early years are a blank, but I know this place."

"Fuck." He stood and paced to the door and back again. "You think you're…"

"I don't think… I don't *know*…" I shook my head. "Do you think it's possible that I could be her? Could I be Coral Clarke?"

3

JOSIAH

I STARED at the stunning woman who sat on Coral's bed, her dark hair tucked behind her ear. With the teddy bear in her arms, she looked almost vulnerable. That was an illusion. I knew better. She stood up to me without flinching. The woman had backbone.

She also had some wild fucking ideas.

I snatched the bear from her and placed it back against Coral's pillow.

"You need to leave." I shattered the rapport I let myself start to feel and slammed my walls back up hard. I shouldn't have let her in here. I should have taken my nails and insisted she leave. She was trespassing on private property as it was. And trespassing on private *matters*.

I ignored her wince as she pushed herself to her

feet. Whatever was going on, it was none of my business, just like Coral Clarke was not hers. Fucking city girl coming up here, to my home. Trying to get under my skin. I didn't know what agendas she had and I didn't give a shit. She needed to do what everyone else did, leave me the fuck alone.

"I just thought, if it's—" she started.

"You don't know what you're saying," I snapped. "Get the hell out and don't come back up here. For the last time: stay. The fuck. Away. From. Me."

I would have turned and walked out then and there, but I needed to be sure she left. Women like this, they thought they could do whatever they liked. She'd probably rifle through the house, trying to come up with some reason to be here.

"What if I'm right?" she asked softly.

"You're not." Since she was continuing to be stubborn, I grabbed her wrist and pulled her toward the front door.

"Why not?" She stepped out, but turned to face me as I firmly locked the door. "It would explain why I know about this place. I knew what that room looked like before I stepped foot in it."

I moved toward her, trying to intimidate her with my height and size. I could have picked her up, thrown her into the creek, and barely raised a sweat.

If she didn't leave soon, I might be tempted to do it. I wasn't the serial killer I joked about being, but she was pushing me past all my limits.

"Why would you want any of that?" I asked, in spite of myself. "You know what she must have gone through. You really want that for yourself? Do you know how fucked up that sounds?"

"Who said I *wanted* it?" She lifted her chin and looked me right in the eyes. "Do you think I want to have been kidnapped? Taken away from everyone I cared about? Away from this place." She spread her hands to indicate around her.

"I don't know what you want," I said. The way her eyes flashed made my cock twitch and I hated that. Hated that I wanted her. Hated that I wanted to pin her underneath me and fuck her harder than she'd ever been fucked before. Hated that I wanted her to straddle my hips and ride me until I came inside her. Hated that I let her in, even a little bit.

"I want to know what the truth is." She dropped her hands to her sides.

"The truth is, you're a city girl with a vivid imagination," I said. "That's all. You think this is some kind of fairytale? It's not. You're not a long-lost princess. And I'm not a long lost prince."

"I was thinking *Beauty and the Beast*," she said dryly. "Do you have a library?"

Of course I did. What else would I do with my winter nights up here? Cleaning and maintaining these cottages, and the lodge, took my daylight hours. I needed something to do after sunset. I told her none of that. She was encouraged enough as it was.

"Do you hear that? Your boyfriends are calling you." I tucked the keys back into my pocket and stalked away to my own little house.

"Now I get it," she said after me. "You're Superman and this is the Fortress of Solitude. That explains the super hearing."

I snorted and went on walking, without looking back over my shoulder. I wasn't super anything. If I had the superhero's speed, I would have been able to stop them from taking Coral.

Instead, I relived that moment over and over. Hands on her as they shoved her into the back of the dark blue sedan. A glint of sunlight on the roof as they drove away, bright enough to force me to cover my eyes. There was no squeal of tyres. No roar of the engine. They just took her and left. Not in a hurry, but still faster than I could run.

I didn't need super hearing to hear the door of

her car close before she also drove away. Finally. Only when I couldn't hear her vehicle anymore, I turned to watch the last of the dust settle back into place.

Silence crowded in from all four sides, only broken by the light breeze through the canopy. And the sound of the creek as it meandered past, mocking me, because the water knew my secret, but didn't care to share it with anyone else. It wouldn't tell the rest of the world Coral hadn't fallen in and been swallowed by the current.

No, the creek was even better at keeping secrets than I was.

I shook my head at my own thoughts and pushed open the heavy timber door to my house. The silence was thicker here. Since my parents retired and left, it seemed to hang like an oversized blanket. It should have been comforting, but it was smothering at the same time. After Leah's visit, it seemed even more oppressive.

Sometimes I thought about leaving the mountain. Starting over and never looking back. Going where no one knew me, or what happened. Find a place I could live a normal life.

Then I reminded myself of the promise I made. Everyone else could think she was dead if that made them feel better. I was going to keep believing other-wise. Until I decided differently, I was going to maintain her house and her room.

I turned on the old coffee maker and made myself a sandwich. While I ate, I kept half an eye on the window. I wouldn't put it past Leah to turn up again and have a look around.

Why had she thought she might be Coral? Okay, she guessed a few details, but she didn't look like Gavin Clarke, or his wife. Ex-wife; whatever. Not what I could remember much about Susan Clarke anyway. She was quiet and tended to keep to herself. She had Coral on a short leash up until she left. No one ever talked about why she walked away. Not to me anyway. One day she was there and the next day she wasn't.

Like her daughter. The only thing I was certain of was they hadn't left together.

I washed my sandwich down with coffee and remembered the nails Leah brought up with her. I rinsed my dishes and hurried outside to find them. It didn't take me long, they lay in the dirt, right beside the spot where she'd fallen to her knees. The place when she'd knelt, looking back at me with her face ashen. Lips apart, eyes wide.

Stop thinking about her on her knees, I told myself.

Picturing her made me hard. That was too many kinds of fucked up. Even if Connor and Riley weren't involved with her, she wasn't going to involve herself with me. I wouldn't let her. She wouldn't want to be stuck up here, ostracised from everyone. The silence would drive her crazy in a day or two. The sideways glances every time she went into Aurora Hollow to buy groceries. The accusing looks and curled lips. She deserved better than that.

A small part of me, tucked away where I could barely acknowledge it, said maybe I deserved better than that too. I shoved that away, hard. If I'd got Coral to help me with the raking... If I'd run faster, shouted louder...

No, I'd earned the animosity, the sneers, the reflection I hated whenever I looked in the mirror.

I leaned over to pick up the bag and carry it to my workshop. She'd never know, but I was grateful she took the time to drive the nails up here. I hated going into town. If I ever forgot for a moment how they felt about me, all I had to do was step through any doorway. The townsfolk would soon remind me.

I set the nails down on my work bench and smoothed a hand over the top of the dollhouse I was making. This one had tiny shutters, and doors and windows that worked. The blue roof was a change for me. Usually they were green, brown or grey. I liked this colour; it reminded me of Leah's eyes.

I picked up a small wooden chair and checked the paintwork on the back and arms. I'd had to touch up a couple of sections that weren't exactly how I wanted them, but they were better now. Satisfied, I placed them in a box, along with the rest of the tiny furniture. Including a fridge and microwave, all made by hand.

I carried the dollhouse out to my truck and placed the box beside it. Roping everything down, I tied a firm knot to keep it all from moving, and climbed into the driver's seat.

With loud, classic rock coming through the speakers, I navigated the bends down the mountain, through Aurora Hollow, until the land became flat. For kilometre after kilometre, there was nothing until I reached my destination. A larger town, surrounded by farmland. Big enough for a stranger to step foot in town without the gossip train doing the rounds in sixty seconds flat. I could walk around here for a short time without notice. A short time was all I needed.

I parked in front of a flat building, climbed out and untied the dollhouse and box and tossed the rope down on the bed. Lifting them out of the back of the truck, I left the toys where I always did, beside the door. No note, no fanfare. Everything would be given to a kid in need. Someone who had nothing else to play with. Someone who'd appreciate the hours I put into making all of this. A kid who needed something to smile at.

Not for thanks. Not for money. Just in the hope it would help to lessen my guilt for a little while. Making all of the delicate things kept my mind off everything else. It gave me a purpose even I recognised was more healthy than maintaining a kid's bedroom. I knew I could have sold what I made, but I liked it better this way.

Before anyone could step out and see me, I hurried back to my truck and drove away. I was almost certain someone watched, but they never said a word. Instead, respecting my privacy and need to remain anonymous. Besides, who would believe them? Not anyone in my hometown. No, they'd refuse the gift. That's why I brought them down here.

In Aurora fucking Hollow, they'd probably throw it all on a fire and burn it to ashes. It wouldn't help. Wouldn't make them feel better. It wouldn't change how they felt about me. They'd still hate my guts.

After so long, I should be used to it. I shouldn't care anymore.

Sometimes I pretended I didn't. I provoked them, just to piss them off. I liked seeing them get angry.

It was better than being ignored.

"You're getting soft," I told myself as I headed out of town. Maybe I was, because it didn't matter what I did. Nothing dulled the guilt when I recalled the look of fear in her eyes before they stuffed her in the car and took her. I should have been able to keep her safe. I failed her and for that I'd never forgive myself. I didn't deserve forgiveness from anyone else.

What would things be like if I'd kept her close to me? If I'd sat beside her instead of raking leaves? My dad would have yelled at me for leaving work undone, but then they couldn't have taken her. I would have had a chance of fighting them off while she ran to her own father. Or made things more difficult so they didn't take her. Something. Anything. She'd still be around, living life the way she was supposed to.

And I wouldn't be so fucking lonely.

4

LEAH

"Where have you been?" Connor leaned against the front of my cottage, beside the door. Riley next to him.

"I'm surprised you didn't make yourself comfortable inside," I remarked. Since they had a key, they could let themselves in whenever they liked. And they did. Their personal favourite? When I was in the bath.

"We wouldn't want to intrude on your privacy." Connor smirked.

I barked a laugh. "Since when?" I pulled out my key and unlocked the door before stepping inside. I didn't bother to invite them in, they'd invite themselves anyway.

"Since it's not as much fun in here if you're not

here," Riley said. He closed the door behind him and followed me and Connor to the kitchen.

"It's nice to see you have some boundaries." I turned on the coffee machine and leaned my back against the kitchen counter. "I was starting to think you had none."

"We don't have many and the line is narrow." Connor cupped my cheek and leaned in to brush his lips over mine. "You didn't answer the question."

I decided it was better to rip the Band-Aid off and be done with it. "I was up at Josiah's. He left something in town, a bag of nails, so I took it up to him."

Predictably, both of their bodies stiffened, harder than steel.

"You went where?" Connor whisper-growled. "Why would you go near him? He would have come back to town sooner or later."

"You don't want him in town," I pointed out. They made that abundantly clear from the day we met.

"We want him in town more than we want you near him," Riley said. "Did he touch you?" He looked ready to grab a kitchen knife and confront Josiah if he had.

"If he touched me, it would be because I wanted him to," I said evenly. "But no, he didn't touch me." I wasn't sure how to explain the rest of the encounter.

"So you dropped off nails and left?" Connor squinted at me, his jaw tight.

I could have agreed with him and left it at that, but I decided to be honest. Besides, I wanted to work through my thoughts. That would be easier if I said the words out loud.

"I feel like I've been there before. Everything about the place was familiar." I tucked hair behind my ear and let my mind wander back.

"Have you been up there since you arrived in town?" Riley asked.

Slowly, I shook my head. "No. The farthest I've been are the falls, and that was with both of you. Josiah, he let me look in Coral's house. In her bedroom."

"The fucker—" Connor started, his face turning red.

I placed my hands on his chest. "It's not like that. I thought I remembered her room. Is it possible someone filmed in there and I saw it on TV or on the Internet?"

"If it happened I don't know about it," Connor said after a moment's thought. "Why would they? She drowned. Why would they show her room?"

"Because maybe she didn't drown," I said. "I know you don't want to think Josiah was telling the truth, but what if he was? What if she was taken that day?"

"If they thought that was what happened and filmed in her bedroom and some attempt to… I don't know, find her, wouldn't they have told everyone in town?" Riley asked.

I nodded slowly. "Yeah, I guess they would. That doesn't mean she wasn't taken. There's one explanation for why I felt like everything up there was familiar."

"You're psychic?" Riley frowned at me. "Did you touch her things? Maybe you can lead the police to her remains."

"What the fuck, bro?" Connor turned to give him a funny look. "You don't believe that stuff, do you?"

Riley shrugged one shoulder. "I don't know. A lot happens in this world I can't explain. Why both of you like me is one of them."

"Because you're cute," I said. He had his moments, but I was becoming more and more attached to both of them.

Riley elbowed Connor. "Did you hear that? I'm cute."

Connor rolled his eyes but a smile was tugging at the corners of his mouth. "Leah, don't encourage him." He blew out a long breath between pursed lips. "Okay, why do you think it was familiar to you?"

"This is going to sound crazy," I said tentatively. "But what if I am Coral Clarke?"

Both of them stared at me.

"Whatever bullshit Josiah has going on in your head, you need to forget it," Connor said after a few beats of uncomfortable silence. "Coral Clarke is dead. Put that out of your mind and stay away from him."

"Or else what?" I shoved his chest, but he didn't move.

He caught my wrists and held them tight. "Or we'll fuck those thoughts out of your pretty little head. Get on..." He stopped himself and looked down at my knees. Or the front of my jeans which were covered in dirt where I'd fallen to them.

He turned toward my bedroom and pulled me with him, leaving Riley to follow behind. Connor sat me down on the edge of my bed and stepped between my legs.

"Take out my cock," he growled. "I'm going to fuck your mouth until you don't remember his name or hers."

"What if I say no?" I asked, lifting my chin defiantly. He knew that tone of voice. If I really meant no, he'd step away. I liked to challenge him and Riley. It made things more interesting.

Connor grabbed a fistful of hair and tugged my head back until I was looking right at him.

"Take. Out. My. Cock. Now."

A smile on my lips, I pushed down the front of his track pants and boxers, letting his thick erection spring free.

"Open your mouth," he ordered.

My eyes on his, I did what he said, letting him press his tip against my tongue. I licked around his head, tasting pre-cum as it leaked from his slit.

Without another word, he pushed himself all the way in, to the back of my throat. His hand still in my hair, he started to thrust, nudging the back of my throat each time. Smiling every time I gagged.

"Good girl," he said between thrusts. "You like that, don't you? Me fucking your mouth. This pretty little mouth was made for me. And Riley."

Riley sat down beside me. "You want Josiah to fuck your mouth too, don't you? You want him to come inside you so you can swallow him down." He ran the back of his hand down my cheek. "And your stepbrother too? I saw the look on your face when you thought you saw him at the fall festival. You would have fucked him amongst the trees after you fucked me."

I swivelled my eyes toward him. What expression did I have on my face? I was confused at seeing him there. Wondering why the hell he was in town. Okay, maybe there was some physical attraction I hadn't admitted to myself. A subconscious desire to be bent over and have him fill me up from behind.

"See?" Riley whispered in my ear. "I saw the way your eyes darkened. You want all of us to fuck you. Tell me something, sweetheart. Do you want all four of us to fuck you at the same time?"

"Riley," Connor said warningly.

"Just asking our woman what she wants," Riley said unapologetically. "If she wants all her holes filled, then that's what she should get." He turned back to me. "Let's see how this would go. Connor in your mouth. Josiah… He should have your pussy. I can take your ass. And Brooks? He might like one of our asses. Or maybe he and I can both share your pussy. Would you like that?" He brushed hair off the side of my face. "Two cocks together in your tight little pussy."

He pushed his hand down between my thighs,

over the front of my jeans. That was almost enough to make me come on the spot.

"She likes that idea, Con," Riley said. "We should make it happen."

Connor grunted. "After I come in her mouth." His thrusts became quicker now, more frantic until he came, squirting hot cum into the back of my throat, forcing me to swallow quickly.

He slid out of me slowly and took a step back. His now-flaccid, but still impressive cock hung between his thighs.

"Fuck her," he said simply.

"Yes please." Riley had both of our clothes off in a matter of moments, tossing garments this way and that, and ran his hands up and down my body. "How do you want me to fuck her?"

Connor thought for a moment. "So I can see you."

Riley gripped my hips and drew me to him, so we sat face to face. He draped my legs over his and positioned my entrance right in front of his cock. "Can you see?"

"Yeah, I can." Connor had his phone out and was standing beside me so he could film us as Riley pulled me onto his cock, filling me to the brim. "That's perfect."

He had a thing for filming us, but as far as I knew, he hadn't shared it with anyone. He better not. This was private, just for us. How many times had he watched the videos he filmed? How did I look in them? I wondered, but I wasn't game enough to ask, not yet. I was self-conscious enough without seeing myself fucking and being fucked. Naked and sweating, sometimes decorated with cum.

"Perfect is the word." Riley half closed his eyes and slid out of me before slamming back in. "You feel incredible. If I could, I'd stay like this forever. Buried deep inside you."

"You feel incredible too," I said. Both of them made me feel so good, so full. I raised my hands and rubbed them up and down over my nipples, making them hard.

At the same time, Riley put a hand between us, teasing my clit with his thumb while he thrust in and out with even, firm strokes.

"Close your eyes and pretend it's Josiah's hand on your pussy," Riley whispered. "And Brooks inside you. What would you tell them?"

"I'd tell them not to stop," I said, groaning the last word. I pictured Brooks lying over me, Josiah's hand between us. Dark-haired and blonde, but both muscular, their bodies chiselled works of art.

I hadn't seen either of them naked, but I'd imagined it enough times. I'd bet the reality was even better. I never wanted to see them as much as I did right now. If both of them were here, I'd give myself to them. Let them fuck my body and beg them to come inside me. I wanted the image Riley painted, all four of them fucking me at once.

"What else would you say?" Riley rubbed me a little faster. "What would you think? Would you think 'my stepbrother is fucking me?' 'My stepbrother has his cock inside my pussy?'"

Every word made me hotter than the last. His dirty mouth was driving me absolutely wild.

I could barely form words, but I managed a strained, "Yes."

"Say it," Connor insisted. "Tell us you want your stepbrother to fuck you."

"I want..." I was so close to coming. "I want my stepbrother to fuck me." The moment the words were out of my mouth, I came against Riley's hand, while picturing Josiah's fingers there instead. Brooks' cock hard inside me.

"Good girl," Riley said with a grunt. "Fuck, fuck, fuck..." He groaned out his own orgasm as he came inside me, thrusting faster, milking every drop of his release. "So fucking good."

He slumped forward, panting lightly. "We need to make that happen. I want to watch both of them fuck you. Then Connor and I will."

I responded to that in the only way I could.

"Yes please."

5

LEAH

AFTER THE GUYS LEFT, I had a quick shower and walked next door to knock on Fiona's door. No answer; she must be out somewhere. I thought about wandering over to Whitney's or Holly's, but I went the other way and headed into town instead.

Walking in no particular direction, I strolled past a couple of people carrying boxes into the town's new bookshop. The shelves were already lined with books; the romance section, featuring a lot of indie authors, being the biggest. I couldn't wait until they opened. I'd probably spend far too much time in there. And too much money as well, but they were books after all.

I remembered the conversation with Josiah about having a library. Did he really? And if he did, how big was it? I decided it was probably huge and went on walking, trying to stay out of the way.

I found myself in front of the Snowdrop Café. Since it was coffee o'clock somewhere in the world, I ducked inside and slid into a seat.

"Leah!" Carly greeted me warmly. "You look fabulous today."

I glanced down at my jeans with the torn knee, and my dark purple t-shirt. "Um, thanks." I hadn't put much thought into what I was wearing. Then again, I usually didn't. On the occasions I did, I found myself wanting to paint. As if somehow the universe preferred me messy.

"What can I get you?" Carly asked.

"I'd love a cup of coffee," I said. "But I don't suppose you have time for a couple of questions?"

"Since it's quiet in here, I think I can make time," she said. "Let me get us both a coffee." She hurried away, returning a couple of minutes later with a cup in each hand. She slid into the chair opposite me and pushed one over, cupping her hands around the other one.

"What's on your mind?" she asked. She cocked her head, looking genuinely interested.

I saw no reason to beat about the bush. "Josiah Lachance."

Carly nodded slowly. "Ah. Are you and he..."

"No," I said quickly. "We're— I'm not sure what we are. Friends, maybe?" I exhaled slowly out my nose. "I think he needs some."

"Friends? Yes, I'd say you're right. I always try to give him a few minutes when he's in town, but he rarely drops in here." She sipped her coffee.

"Do you remember that day?" I didn't need to elaborate. We both knew what I was referring to. If Carly lived here at the time, she would have been in her early thirties.

"I do." She brushed a handful of curls off the side of her face. "I mean, as much as I could since I was down here in town. I was working at one of the hotels at the time. Cleaning rooms and making beds. I remember seeing a couple of police cars roll into town. Then everyone was saying Coral was gone."

"They searched for her?" I asked. Hadn't the guys told me that when they explained why they hated Josiah so much?

Carly crinkled her brow. "I presume so. The police said they had the matter under control. They wouldn't let any of us up there. I never thought to question why."

"How long after that was it before Gavin Clarke

moved down into town?" I took a sip of my own coffee and tried to play it cool.

"Almost right away," Carly said. "Someone went up there, I think it was Jacob Ferguson. Said Gavin was ranting about losing his baby. He was beside himself. Said he trusted the wrong person. Then she was gone. Jacob brought him to town and they cleaned up the cottage for him."

"Gavin said he trusted Josiah and he shouldn't have?" That felt like a stab right to my own heart.

"I suppose that was what he meant, but I only heard it second or third hand," Carly said. "Gavin didn't talk about it after that. It's like he blocked it from his mind. Can't say I blame him. If she was my kid…" Carly sniffed.

"Right," I said softly. "Why does no one believe Josiah is telling the truth? What if he was?"

"I saw Coral with her father a few times," Carly said softly. "She was a sweetheart. I don't want to think about what might have happened if Josiah was telling the truth."

"What if things weren't so bad for her?" I asked. "She might have had a happy childhood."

Carly looked doubtful. "I'd wish that for her, but… What's with all the questions, anyway? You're not thinking of writing a book about her, are you?"

She wrinkled her nose as though she found the idea distasteful.

"No," I said with a short laugh. "I guess I'm just trying to get my head around a few things."

So many things. Feeling as though her bedroom was familiar was one thing, but putting everything else together was another. If the police searched for her, why was Josiah still so convinced she was taken? I supposed it was possible he was suffering from some kind of mental illness that messed with his memories. The reality might have been so traumatic he blocked it out, replacing it with something easier to take.

I might be suffering from the same thing. Imagining myself as her, growing up with people who loved her, not a family who were indifferent most of the time. I considered opening a gallery in town, but maybe what we really need was a good therapist. Would Josiah see them if they set up practice here? Maybe if he was dragged, kicking and screaming. Chances were, that was what it would take.

"It was a shocking thing to happen," Carly agreed. "Everyone kept a closer eye on all the kids after that. Well, as much as anyone could with some of them being wild." She laughed.

"I think I can guess who you're referring to." I

smiled. Connor and Riley would have gone on doing the same crazy things, regardless. "Can I ask one more question?"

She flapped a hand at me. "Go ahead."

"Josiah's parents. They used to work at the lodge?" I asked.

"That's right," Carly said. "Franco and—"

"Tatiana," I said without thinking.

Carly squinted at me. "Yes, Tatiana. How did you know?"

I placed my coffee cup down on the table. "I don't know, I must have heard it somewhere. What did they think about all of this? They must have been concerned about their son."

"Honestly, they always kept to themselves," Carly said after a moment's thought. "They were busy working. She'd come into town once in a while, but never said much."

"So you don't know if she believed Josiah or not?" I asked. If a mother couldn't believe her own son, then who would? Although, if it was my mother, she'd probably agree with the town and lose no sleep over it. Maybe I wasn't giving her much credit, but that was how I felt.

"No idea," Carly admitted. "If I recall someone said they asked her once and she changed the subject. We can be a nosy bunch, but we also know when to keep our noses out of other people's business. Some of the time." She raised her eyebrows and smiled.

"It would be a difficult subject to talk about, I suppose," I said.

"Absolutely," Carly agreed. "I can say this, though. Tatiana Lachance adores her son. So does Franco. It wouldn't surprise me if they believed him, but said nothing because they knew no one would listen." She twisted her mouth to the side in frustration. She loved the town, but saw its flaws as well.

"I hope they did," I said sincerely. "He seems lonely up there." He'd be the last one to admit that, but in those few moments where we almost got along with each other, he seemed to enjoy the connection. He might not even be aware of how much he needed it.

"If I didn't know better, I'd think you have a thing for him," she teased.

I picked my cup back up, inhaling the delicious smell. "Maybe I do."

"Someone should," she said. "But be careful. This town can be…very small sometimes." She swivelled her eyes back and forth as if we might have people spying on us right here in the middle of the café.

Apart from us, only two other people were here, sitting by the wall in quiet conversation. They hadn't taken their eyes off each other since I arrived. No, they weren't watching us.

"I've noticed that," I said, with no judgement. For the most part, the town welcomed me with open arms. They included me in just about every aspect of life here. In return, everyone knew everyone's business, including mine. Most of the time, that wasn't a bad thing. I wasn't doing anything scandalous after all. Unless they'd be scandalised by my relationship with Riley and Connor. If they were, that was their problem.

"I should get back to work." Carly downed the last of her coffee, patted the tabletop and stood.

"Thank you for taking the time to talk to me," I said. "I appreciate it."

"Any time," she said with a smile. "I heard a rumour you might be opening a gallery in town. I look forward to it."

I assumed Louisa told her. The mayor seemed to like the idea, but that's all it was for now. An idea. I needed more art and money before I could even consider renting space and fitting it out to accommodate all the work I wanted to put on display. Mine and other's. I wanted to put Aurora Hollow on the art scene map. I wanted the town to be a place where people could make art as well as buy it.

We were surrounded by so much inspiration here, it was perfect. I meant it when I told Josiah the Clarke house would make a perfect retreat and gallery. It really would. Quiet and picturesque. I could sit up there for an entire year and never get tired of drawing and painting the landscape. Not to mention looking around for the perfect sticks and logs to turn into sculptures. That was a habit that wouldn't leave, even if I wanted it to. An artist's mind was difficult to quiet. Impossible to silence. We were always thinking about creating the next piece.

"If I do, I'll invite you to the grand opening," I assured her.

"Wild horses couldn't keep me away." Smiling, she hurried away into the kitchen, leaving me alone with my thoughts.

Those were tumultuous. If there was a possibility I was Coral Clarke, then Gavin was my father. If he was, then what did that mean? My mother told me my father left when I was little. Had she lied to me about that? Was she even my mother? If she lied about that, then what else had she lied about? Was anything in my life real?

I felt like my whole existence was tipped upside

down. Nothing made sense anymore. If she wasn't my mother, then who was she? One thing I knew for sure, she'd never done anything inappropriate to me. Neither had my stepfather. Or anyone else, that I could remember. They were disinterested.

I rubbed my temples slowly. I wasn't sure where I'd even start to get answers to all of my questions. Of those, I had a ton. They seemed to reproduce by the moment. If one was answered, two or three more popped up.

Including one in particular. Did I really want to know the truth? What good would it do now?

It would clear Josiah's name for one, but would he care? If it was me, I would, but he seemed to enjoy playing the anti-hero. He might find some other reason for people to dislike and reject him.

The bell over the door tingled as someone stepped inside.

I looked up and my mouth dropped open.

"Brooks?"

6

BROOKS

I STARED BACK at my stepsister, who sat with her lips apart, blue eyes on me. Her face haunted my dreams for too fucking long. The amount of times I thought about her, with my fist around my cock, hating myself afterward... Of all the women I ever met, why did she keep clinging to my attention like she belonged there? The fact I was here at all, in the same town as her...

"Leah," I said coldly. "What a surprise."

She rose from her chair like a cat, all smooth and feline. With a hint of the stiffness she tried to hide from everyone. She couldn't hide it from me. I knew her too well. Knew when she was uncomfortable. The way the side of her mouth pulled back slightly was her tell, every time. Stubborn bitch.

"What are you doing here?" She walked toward me like she couldn't believe I was standing in front of her.

"I thought I'd get a coffee." I stepped past her and gave the server a wave.

"That wasn't what I meant," she said to my back. "Why are you in Aurora Hollow?"

"One coffee and a sandwich," I said to the server. "Thanks."

"Brooks." Leah placed a hand on my shoulder. "If you've come to—"

Was she trying to threaten me?

I turned around, letting her hand fall away from me. "It's a free country. I can be here if I want." I would have loved to see her flinch, but that wasn't her style. Leah Kent never backed down, not from me. No matter how hard I pushed.

"And yet, it's a hell of a coincidence," she said sarcastically. "You happen to turn up in the same town I'm living in."

I rolled my eyes. "There's no such thing as coincidence." She knew that as well as I did.

"Which brings me back to why you're here." She raised her chin, daring to provoke me. One of these days she would, and I wouldn't be responsible for what I'd do to her. Once I started, I wouldn't be able to stop.

"Because I wanted to," I said. "This town is interesting." I took my coffee and sandwich from the server, slipped her some money and turned to walk out.

"Broo—" Her annoyed voice cut off as the door closed behind me. The tinkle of the bell told me she opened it again to follow me out. "What the hell?"

I continued to ignore her, instead walking to the edge of town, where I found a quiet spot with a thick trunk to sit against while I tried to eat my sandwich. Like always, she was a dog with a bone, following me, as if she didn't dare let me out of her sight.

"You're such a prick." She sat down beside me.

"You already knew that about me." I bit into my sandwich, washing it down with a cup of coffee. "This coffee is terrible."

"Then I guess you better go back to the city, where you can get better coffee," she said snidely.

I pretended to consider that for a few moments, the cup pressed against my lower lip.

"I like it here," I said finally. "I think I'll stick around for a while." I took another bite. At least the sandwich was edible. Mostly.

"Why?" she asked insistently. "You don't even like

getting dirt on your shoes. Why would you want to stick around a place like this?"

"Someone has to keep an eye on you," I told her. "Look what happened when Mom and Dad looked away for a moment. You ran away to the mountains."

She bristled, like I knew she would.

"Since when do you call her Mom?" Her eyes were narrowed, flashing with annoyance.

Exactly never, but she didn't need to know that. Let her think things changed in her absence.

"What are you doing here?" I asked her. "This isn't exactly the sculpture capital of the world." I knew that would also get her going. She made herself too easy a target for my barbs. As I expected, her eyes glazed with unshed tears.

"You're an asshole," she said. "For your information, I've been painting and working."

"Who for?" I finished off my sandwich and coffee and stuffed the paper into the empty cup.

"My boyfriends," she said, her chin dropped almost to her chest.

I burst out laughing. "Sorry, I thought you said boyfriends, plural."

She tipped her head back, looking directly at me. "I did say that. Connor and Riley have been good to me." She looked as though she was going to add something else, but pressed her lips together.

I snorted. "I bet they have. Let me guess, you've been good to them too." I wanted to strangle both of them for touching her. Why would she let them do that when she wouldn't let me close enough?

"We've been good to each other," she said unapologetically. "Maybe you should try it sometime."

Before she could blink, I had my hand around her throat, the pressure just enough to make her eyes widen.

"Maybe I should," I said, my voice pitched low. "Maybe I should try you."

She swallowed, her throat constricting under my palm, but made no move to pull away.

"Is that what you want?" I whispered.

Her tongue slid over her lip. "I want to know why you're here in town."

Her panties were drenched, I could tell by the look in her eyes. If she thought I wouldn't fuck her here beside the road with cars driving back and forth, she was wrong. But I didn't want it this easily. I wanted her to keep fighting me. I wanted her to go on hating me while I slammed into her. I wanted her to hate herself for doing it. Only then would I know I'd won.

"I wanted to see where you went," I said. "You didn't think you could disappear and I wouldn't notice, did you?" If she did, she was very much mistaken.

"How did you know I was here?" She swallowed again, but still didn't move away.

I smiled. The kind of smile that makes people shiver without knowing why. Not a nice or warm expression. I didn't do nice or warm. I hadn't since the day I met her.

"I have a tracker on your car," I said. "And one in an app on your phone. I know exactly where you are and when, and for how long. I know who you call, and you haven't called your mother." I clicked my tongue. "I should punish you for that." I lowered my hand from her throat and let my words sink in.

"You've been tracking me?" She shook her head slowly. "For how long?" I could see her mind ticking over, thinking frantically. As if she'd done things she was scared I knew about.

"Since shortly after we met," I said easily, as if that wasn't completely fucked up. "I also had a camera in your bedroom back home."

I leaned in and whispered, "I know which is your

favourite vibrator. I've watched you getting off so many times."

Her face paled slightly. I expected her to slap me and call me names. Threaten me with the police, or to tell her mother or my father.

"If you were watching so closely, then why didn't you come in and help me?" She raised one of her perfectly shaped eyebrows a fraction.

I have to admit her question took me by surprise. I didn't like surprises. I wanted her to squirm. Instead, she seemed even more aroused.

"Why would I want to touch you?" I hedged.

"Why else would you watch me?" she countered. "You wanted to see me come, why not do it yourself?"

My brain finally caught up. "You knew." Fuck. "You knew and you did it anyway."

"I suspected," she admitted. "You gave me that jewellery box. You'd never given me anything before. I looked it over carefully. Found what I thought might be a camera. Figured you're too much of a selfish asshole to share with any of your friends. So I gave you a show. The next morning, you looked smug as fuck, which confirmed what I suspected. You'd watched every moment."

She smiled slowly. "Did you enjoy the show?"

I had to think quickly, gather my thoughts. I wasn't going to let her get one up on me. How had I not realised she knew I was watching? That her sweet and innocent act was just an act. The real performance happened on top of her covers, where she'd slid the vibrator into her pussy over and over until she brought herself to orgasm.

"It could use some work," I said finally, throwing in a half-shrug as if I wasn't rattled.

She laughed out loud. "There's always room for improvement. Before you ask, yes, my boyfriends like to film me too." She really didn't seem at all concerned by that, or the possibility of the footage being shared with the entire world. She must trust those pricks. If they released any of it, they'd have me to answer to. I wouldn't hesitate to wring their necks.

"Leah Kent, porn star." I smirked. "I should have known. You look sweet, but deep down you're a slut."

She didn't look bothered by the accusation. She knew she'd taken me by surprise and was smug as fuck about it. But I'd taken her by surprise too, tracking her car. I could call that a tie, but I hated ties.

"Is that why you're really here?" she asked. "You missed your entertainment?"

"Something like that," I said. I pushed myself up to my feet and brushed my hands on each other. I had hours of footage recorded I could watch any time I wanted to. All stored somewhere no one else could access it. Every moment of that was for my eyes only.

"This has been an interesting conversation." She struggled a little to stand, but I watched without offering to help. I smiled as though it amused me, but the truth was she wouldn't accept anyway. Leah Kent was as stubborn as they came.

"We've only just started," she said. "About the tracker in my car—"

"It stays there," I said. "In case I need to know where you are." She could buy a new car and I'd put one in that as well. She wasn't driving anywhere without me knowing. No matter what she did, that was non-negotiable.

"I'm going to find the one on my phone and delete it," she said as if that was some kind of win.

"I figured you would." If I cared about that, I wouldn't have told her it was there. It had outlived its usefulness anyway. Since she hardly called anyone, there was nothing to discover.

In a town this small, I could keep my eyes on her personally, any time I wanted to. Like when she was on the Ferris wheel with those two other men. Were those her boyfriends? I presumed so. Whatever, I wasn't threatened by them. I'd turned and walked away because I wasn't ready to speak to her yet. I wanted her to know I was in town, nothing more. I'd stepped back behind the food trucks and watched her run around, looking for me before giving up. The whole thing was fucking hilarious.

"Don't you want to know why I didn't tell my mother or your father that you've been watching me?" she asked.

I laughed at that. "I already know the answer. They wouldn't have believed you. And if they had, they wouldn't have given a shit. They didn't care what either of us did."

Her brow creased. "That's not true. They care what you do. You were always the one they—"

"They fucking did not," I snarled, keeping my voice low still. Without waiting to see her response, I turned and stalked away.

This time, she didn't follow me.

7

LEAH

I WATCHED HIM WALK AWAY, shook my head and
started back to my place. If I thought my mind was
in turmoil before, it was worse now. He'd been
tracking me? Monitoring my movements for years?
How had I not realised the extent of his scrutiny?
Watching me come was one thing. A private,
arousing secret. I had no way of knowing when he
watched, but I'd thought about him every time.
Assumed he was there on the other side of the
camera.

Why hadn't I turned the camera away from
myself? Because I didn't hate him watching, and
because he'd know I knew. He could have removed
the camera and replaced it with one I didn't know
about. Was that the only camera he had watching

me? I suspected it was. If there were more, he would have been crowing about it.

What did it say about me that I let him watch something so private? I supposed it was my way of dealing with the attraction I had for him, that otherwise had no outlet. Apart from that, he'd shown me no interest.

"This whole thing is fucked up," I said to myself. Mindful I might suffer for it later, I hurried over to Connor's small stone house and tapped on the door.

Heavy footsteps sounded from inside before the door was swung open.

"Let me guess, you missed me?" Connor lounged against the door, looking smug.

"She missed us," Riley called out from deep inside.

"I might have," I said evasively. I did, though. I got more and more attached to both of them by the day. If I was honest with myself, I was falling for them. They could be possessive assholes, but they looked out for me. Make sure I had everything I needed. No one else had done that for me before. I wouldn't offend them by calling them sweet, but they had their moments.

"I was wondering if either of you knew how to find a tracking device on a car?"

Connor stared at me for a moment before grabbing my wrist and pulling me inside.

"What the hell are you talking about?" He closed the door behind us. "If Josiah—"

I put a hand on his chest. "This isn't about Josiah. It's about my stepbrother, Brooks." I quickly explained about the tracker on my car and the app on my phone.

Riley put his hand out until I placed my phone on his palm. He opened it using the pin code. He must have watched me and memorised it.

These men.

He squinted at the screen and swiped until he found what he was looking for. "There, deleted. Very subtle, masking that as a news app. Those things are notoriously difficult to delete. And tend not to get noticed." He handed the phone back.

"I might have noticed if I knew it was there." I pushed my phone back into my pocket. "About my car?"

"That could be trickier." Connor's brows knitted. "We can take a look. If you want us to." He hooked an arm around me and pulled me to him. "You might get off on having another possessive man around."

I swallowed, unsure if I should tell him about the jewellery box camera and exactly how much of me

Brooks had seen. These two might throw him over the Aurora Falls if they didn't like what they heard.

"Out with it," Connor insisted. "What did the fucker do?" He looked as though he might deal with Brooks regardless of what I said.

"Did you fuck him?" Riley asked. He looked disappointed. Not at the idea that I was with someone else, but at the thought he wasn't there to watch.

These men and their watching.

"No, I did not fuck him," I said clearly. I closed my eyes, took a deep breath and told them everything else.

"He was stalking you?" Connor looked at me sideways, clearly not having made up his mind about how he felt about that.

"I… I suppose you could call it that," I said uncertainly. When he put it that way, I should probably be more worried about Brooks' behaviour than I was. He liked to try to provoke me, but I didn't think he meant any specific harm.

"Is it wrong that I think it's hot he was watching?" Riley asked, wincing. "I mean, if I was Leah's stepbrother, I'd also watch."

"You would fucking not," Connor told him. "You'd go in there and fuck her. So would I."

"You're right," Riley conceded. "Brooks has more restraint than I do. When you think about it, that's pretty impressive. He must have a really muscular hand."

I couldn't help laughing at that. Thinking about Brooks being sexually frustrated from watching me was…honestly, his own fault.

"He never made a move on you?" Connor asked.

"Never," I said. I sank down on Connor's couch, a dark grey sectional that contrasted with the rustic vibe of the rest of the place. Not to mention the pale, floral wallpaper that looked as though it had decorated the walls for longer than I'd been alive.

"What I can't understand is *why* he did it. I've always thought he hated me. Why would he want to watch me get off?"

Riley sat beside me. "Have you seen yourself? Even if I hated you, I'd want to watch you orgasm. You're fucking hot."

"Riley's right." Connor perched on the coffee table. "I couldn't stand you when I first met you, but I still wanted to fuck you. I know vice versa is true." He flicked his finger back and forth between me and himself.

"When we first met, fucking wasn't my initial reaction to you," I said dryly. "Flipping you off and proving to you that you couldn't force me to leave town is more accurate."

Connor snorted. "All of that while you were wet for me, honey. You don't have to admit it, we all know it's true."

"No one could ever accuse you of having a tiny ego," I teased.

He smirked. "I don't have a tiny anything."

"He has an oversized ego to go with his oversized cock," Riley said, joining in on the shit disturbing.

"If you're trying to offend me, maybe don't do it by giving me compliments." Connor sat back, looking even more smug.

"What am I going to do with you two?" I shook my head, but smiled.

"You can start by introducing us to Brooks," Riley said. "I want to meet the guy with the audacity to watch our woman getting herself off. And then I want him to watch while I get her off."

"I have no idea where he's staying," I admitted. "He's the one with the tracking device, not me."

"I'll put out feelers," Connor said. "Someone will know where he is. Do you have a picture of him?"

I frowned. "I can probably find one." Taking selfies with each other wasn't something we did. Ever. I pulled out my phone and looked at his social media feed. Frowned. "There should be a photo of him on here somewhere."

All I could find was a handful of pictures from home. A bridge here, squirrel there. Nothing personal and none of any people.

"I think his father has an account." I looked it up and started to scroll.

"What kind of relationship do you have with your stepfather?" Riley asked, clearly trying to be provocative.

I glanced up at him. "Nothing salacious. I can promise you that." I couldn't even remember him so much as giving me a hug, which suited me just fine. His was a radar I didn't care to be on. Strange that Brooks would say he wasn't on it either. Why would the family's golden boy not be noticed?

I looked back down at the phone, scrolling past photos of my mother, people he worked with, his sister and her kids. Finally, I found a photo of him and Brooks standing side-by-side right after he married my mother. They were both smiling, but neither looked happy.

There were no photos of me.

I turned the phone around to show the guys.

"He's kinda hot," Riley said.

Connor grudgingly grunted his agreement. "I'll

keep an eye out for him." He saved the photo and sent a copy to himself and Riley. "We can show that around to folks. The grapevine will do the rest."

"Do me a favour and don't throw him in the lake," I said.

"I make no promises." Connor handed my phone back to me.

"I promise to wait until the lake is frozen enough to cut a hole in it," Riley said with a grin. "And drop him in."

"No murdering anyone," I warned both of them. As if I actually thought they were capable of something like that.

"He wouldn't be worth it," Connor said. "But I don't rule out strongly encouraging him to leave town."

"It didn't work on me," I pointed out.

He rolled his eyes. "You're stubborn as fuck."

"And?" I prompted.

"And... I didn't really want you to leave." He shrugged. "I wanted to see if you could stand up to me."

I gave a sceptical look. "Maybe you have that backward. I wanted to see if you could handle me." I raised an eyebrow at him in challenge.

He leaned in until we were almost nose to nose.

"Honey, I can always handle you." He brushed his lips over mine.

"I knew I should have been more difficult." I wrinkled my nose but kissed him back.

He laughed, his breath warm on my mouth. "I don't see how you could have been more difficult. Isn't that your middle name? Leah Difficult Kent?"

"I thought it was Leah Fucking Kent," Riley offered.

"For your information, Connor Difficult Ferguson and Riley Fucking Crane, my middle name is Amy," I said tartly.

They exchanged grins.

"I think she won that round," Riley said.

"It was time we gave her one." Connor looked back at me. "I'm ready to give her a good, hard one." He grabbed my hands and pulled me to my feet. Leading me over to the side of the couch, he pushed me forward, bending me across the high back.

"Stay like that," he ordered. He reached around to undo the front of my jeans and push them down to my feet. My panties went next.

"Tell me something, did talking to your step-brother about him watching you make you wet?" He nudged my thighs apart and slid his hand between them. Slowly, he moved it up to my pussy, then slid a couple of fingers inside me. "The answer is a definite yes." He slid his fingers up and down insde me and out, moving slowly. Fucking me with his hand.

"She looks good like that," Riley said.

"She's going to look better in a moment." Connor slid his hand out of me and slapped it down on my ass.

I let out a squeak, but I liked the sting the slap left behind.

"You look amazing with my handprint on your ass," Connor said. He slapped me again, a couple of times, then he was pushing his cock inside me. Pressing my body down to the couch with his, he started to slowly thrust in and out of me. His hand found my clit and rubbed while he thrust.

Before either of us could come, he pulled himself away. "Riley, get on your back. Pants off."

Riley hurried to comply, lying down on the couch, his bare cock in his hand.

Connor guided me over to straddle Riley's lap, lowering me all the way down his cock. "Lean forward and stay there."

I did as he ordered, watching him disappear into another room before he reappeared with a tube of lube in his hand. He opened it and smeared a cold dollop on my rear hole. He tossed the tube onto the table and straddle Riley, right behind me.

"Has anyone ever fucked this?" He slid the tip of his finger into my ass.

"Never," I whispered. "Please..." I wanted to feel both of them inside me at the same time. Could I take him? He was big. Big enough to hurt. Big enough that I wanted to try. He'd make me feel so full it would drive me wild. If he didn't break me.

He pushed in another finger, rubbing the lube around while stretching my muscles, readying me for him. Finally, he slid them back out and replaced them with the tip of his cock. Slowly and carefully, he eased himself inside me, giving me time to get used to the feeling of having him there. Pressing until he was all the way in.

"Holy fuck, I can feel both of you." Riley's eyes crossed.

"Me too," Connor said, already breathless. He was still for a minute or two before starting to move, setting the pace for all of us. "You're so fucking tight."

And then we were moving in unison, a rolling of hips, grunting and groaning. Thrusting and sighing.

I was the first to say, "I'm going to come."

"Me too," Riley strained to say.

Connor grunted something unintelligible, but it sounded like agreement.

A moment later, I came, both guys following half a heartbeat later. The whole room echoed with our groans, grunts and moans as we shattered as one, swamped by a tsunami of bliss like nothing I'd ever experienced before.

Eventually, we all came down, puffing and sweating, clinging to each other as if we were one person and not three.

My heart was still racing through my ears when Riley said something which sounded like, "I love you."

8

CONNOR

"We need to find the asshole." I worked the plug open and pushed on the side of the dinghy, letting the air out. The last of the white water rafting tours for the year was done. Like we always did, we inspected each one carefully before deflating it and stacking it away. In spring, we'd re-inflate and inspect them again.

"Which one?" Riley glanced over at me and grinned. "Josiah or Brooks?"

I grunted a laugh. He had a point there.

"Both of them, but I meant Brooks this time. Prick thought he could watch our woman." That didn't sit right with me. Especially since he didn't know she'd already guessed he was doing it.

"She wasn't ours at the time." Riley trod on one of the boats, walking around to force the air out.

I could have refuted that, but it wasn't the point.

"He still did it without her permission," I said.

"You have a key to her house without her permission." He jumped off the boat and leaned over to fold it.

"That's different," I said.

"How is it different?" He pushed the folded boat aside and started to flatten another one.

"Because us having a key is in her best interest," I said. "She might need us to come inside when she can't open the door herself. What he did was just fucking creepy."

Riley stopped and looked over at me. "Are you pissed off you didn't think of it first?"

"No," I scoffed. "Why would I want to watch her get off when I can get her off myself?" Anyone could sit back and watch.

"When you put it that way, it is creepy." Riley went back to deflating. "Why do you think he's in town?"

"For her." That was the only thing I was certain of. "He's come to claim her, but he's in for a surprise. We aren't giving her up without a fight."

"Hell no we aren't," Riley agreed. "If he wants her,

he's going to have to share." He levelled a look at me. "How do you feel about that? Sharing her with him." After a beat he added, "And Josiah."

"You want that, don't you?" I asked. I'd heard his dirty talking when we were fucking Leah. He'd all but invited both guys into bed with us.

"I want… I want her to get everything she wants," he said slowly. "And I want her and you. If having her means sharing with them, then yeah, I want that. Nice deflection, by the way. What do you want?"

I released a long sigh. "Do you think maybe she's right? About Coral Clarke. What if things didn't go down the way we were told?"

"Are you admitting there's a chance Josiah wasn't lying?" Riley cocked his head at me. "I noticed you deflected again." He grinned when I flipped him off. "If we were wrong all this time, that would make it easier to share her with him."

That was typical Riley. He was always faster to forgive and forget than I was. It was going to take time for me to get my head around the idea we may not have anything to forgive. If anything, Josiah would be the one having to forgive us. And our parents for creating the whole narrative and perpetuating it to begin with.

I scrubbed a hand over my face. "This whole thing is fucked up."

"You think she's Coral, don't you?" Riley squinted at me.

"I don't know." I dropped my hand to my side. "The first time I saw her, I was drawn to her. Like, I don't know, I didn't want to look away. I was an asshole to her, but even then I felt like she belonged here. You know?"

"Yeah, I know." He gave me a couple of slaps on my shoulder and started to fold the second boat. "It feels like she's always been here."

He was right about that. She fit in like a missing piece of the puzzle. The bit we didn't know was missing until we met her. Once we had, we didn't know how we'd functioned without her.

"Hypothetically, what if she is Coral Clarke? How do we prove it? Should we try to prove it? Would it change anything if we do? She'd still be the same woman, with the same past. And the same future." I didn't give a shit if her name was Engelbert Clutter-buck. It wouldn't change how I felt about her. It wouldn't change how Riley felt about her. Yeah, I heard what he said when we were fucking. I knew he was saying it to both of us. I didn't know about Leah, but I was too chicken shit to say it back. For now.

"This isn't the answer you want, but we have to leave it up to her," Riley said. "She has to decide if she wants to find out the truth or not. But if she does, a DNA test should do it. If we could get Gavin to agree to have his mouth swabbed. Or blood taken."

"Yeah." He'd have to be lucid enough to consent, but if he was, would we have to explain why it was happening? That might fuck him up even more. This whole situation got more and more fucked up the more I thought about it.

"Fiona or Whitney could probably convince him," Riley said. "Those two could sell sand to someone living in the middle of the desert."

I grunt-laughed. That sounded like Fiona and my sister all right. Especially Whitney. She was the master of getting her own way when she put her mind to it. "I guess we wait and see what Leah wants to do."

I helped Riley fold the last couple of boats and drag them over to the pile. We tossed the paddles on top of them and hung all the lifejackets onto hooks.

"Let's grab some lunch and see if we can find Brooks," I said, wiping my hands on my jeans.

"Sounds like a plan." Riley locked the shed behind us and we headed down the street as the first flurries of snow started to settle.

I caught Riley giving me a sideways look. "What?"

He grinned and said, "I remember when we used to catch snowflakes on our tongues."

"Pretty sure that was last winter." I put out my hand to try to catch a few. Summer felt like only weeks ago. We were barely done with the fall festival and it was snowing. Nothing new for here, but it made the year feel like it flew past.

"And the winter before," he said. "And all the winters since we were kids."

"Basically." I pushed the front door to the Frosty Brew open and stepped inside. The warmth of the pub felt cozy after the cold of the street.

"I thought that would be difficult," Riley said, coming in behind me.

I glanced over my shoulder and followed his gaze to where Brooks sat at a table, his eyes on his phone. A half drunk beer sat in front of him, the condensation leaving a puddle on the table. By the look of it, he hadn't touched it in a while.

"Me too." Back straight, I sauntered over, grabbed the back of the chair opposite him and pulled it out with a scrape of wood on hardwood. My father would have been pissed off if he saw, but he wasn't here right now. Lucky for me.

He glanced up at me and frowned as I sat down.

"Can I help you?" he asked coldly. He was good-looking enough, with his chiselled jaw and blonde hair. He'd look prettier on his knees. His plush lips would look perfect around my cock.

"As a matter of fact, you can," I said, matching his tone. Bettering it, if I was honest. His icy cold could use some work. "You're Leah's stepbrother."

He sat back and regarded me and Riley, who plopped into the chair beside me.

"So what if I am?" he asked. "Why do you—" He cut himself off. "You're her...boyfriends." He didn't use air quotes, but it was implied. And amplified by the curl of his lip when he sneered.

"That's us," Riley said cheerfully. "What do you want with her?" He was smiling, but if anyone thought he wouldn't jump up and slam Brooks' face into the table, they were mistaken. He kept his undercurrent of violence more tightly controlled than I did, but it was still there.

"I could ask you the same thing." Brooks didn't flinch. I had to give him credit for that. "What do you want with my stepsister?"

"We care about her," I said. "We don't want her hurt by some blow-in who's going to leave town when he gets bored of the place."

"Who says I'm leaving?" Brooks crossed his arms and looked smug as fuck.

I know, I've seen that expression in the mirror often enough. I was starting to think Leah had a type.

"Are you?" Riley asked. "We know you watched her getting herself off."

That took Brooks aback. Clearly he hadn't expected her to tell us that. Surprise was replaced with anger, furious at having been caught off guard. He was the kind of guy who liked to think he held all the cards. As far as I was concerned, the only cards he had were jokers. Riley and I held the rest.

"So what if I did?" Brooks' voice was tight. "Leah didn't mind."

"Maybe I mind," I said. "She's our girlfriend. I'll ask again, what do you want with her?"

"He wants to fuck her," Riley said before Brooks could respond. "That's why he's here."

"Isn't that all you want from her?" Brooks retorted. "Her pretty little pussy."

"That isn't all we want from her," Riley said, still keeping his tone light. "Like Connor said, we care about her. She's a special woman; we don't want anyone to hurt her. Including everyone sitting at this table right now." After a moment he added, "Unless it's in a way she likes." He slid me a look, reminding me of slapping her ass. She enjoyed that and so had I.

"I—" Brooks looked uncomfortable.

Before he could finish what he was going to say, Leah stepped over to the table.

"What are all of you doing here?"

9

LEAH

I PULLED my coat tighter around myself and stepped into the pub. I was supposed to be meeting Fiona here for lunch, I hadn't expected to see Connor or Riley, much less them sitting with Brooks. Whatever they were talking about, it didn't seem friendly. I knew that look in Riley's eyes. He was sweet, but he could turn on a dime. Connor was, well, Connor. And Brooks didn't look too happy to be in the middle of what I guessed was a confrontation.

"What are all of you doing here?" I slipped into the chair between Riley and Brooks and rested my elbows on the table. "You're not planning each other's demise, are you?"

"We hadn't quite gotten to that point." Riley

draped an arm over my shoulder and leaned in to kiss my cheek.

"Give us a couple more minutes," Connor said, keeping his eyes on Brooks.

"Your boyfriends are…interesting," Brooks said, returning the look. "They were just welcoming me to town."

"I'm sure they were," I said sarcastically. "No one is tossing anyone over the falls." That seemed to be the go-to, empty threat around here. At least, I thought it was an empty threat.

"I was thinking off the lookout," Connor said with a smirk.

"What do you see in these dickheads?" Brooks slid me a glance. "This one seems okay." He gestured vaguely at Riley.

"You hear that, Connor? He thinks I'm okay." It was Riley's turn to smirk. "I think that means he likes me."

"Of course he likes you," I said. "He'd like both of you if he got to know you."

All three of them looked sceptical at that.

"Depends if we want to or not," Connor said.

"Of course we do." Riley squeezed me tighter. "Because that's what Leah wants, right? For all of us to be friends. Or…more than friends." He gave

Brooks an appreciative look. One that immediately set my blood on fire.

I hadn't imagined them together before, but I was now. I liked what my imagination had to tell me. All that bare, muscular flesh heaving, sweating and groaning. Mouths mashed together, fingers wrapped around each other's cocks.

"Whatever you're thinking, I like it," Riley whispered in my ear. "It's making your cheeks flush and your eyes darken."

My face heated. I hadn't realised it was so obvious. I cleared my throat and forced myself to focus.

"So, now you've all met," I started. I stopped, uncertain where I was going with that line of conversation.

"You told them I watched you," Brooks interrupted.

"I don't want to have any secrets between me and them," I said easily. "Unless you're ashamed of doing it?"

"I'm not ashamed," he snapped. "What else have you told them?"

I frowned. "What else is there to say? You and I never got along. We've never been close. I'm surprised you noticed I left." Apart from being alerted by the tracking device in my car.

Brooks rolled his eyes. "Leah seems to be under the belief her mother and my father cared about me, not her."

"Is that true?" Connor asked him.

"No," Brooks scoffed. "They didn't care about anyone but themselves and each other. Their only interest in me was trying to mould me into what they wanted me to be. They didn't give a shit about me as a person."

"They always—" I started to protest.

He cut me a look, bordering on a glare. "They always fucking what? Let me be whatever I wanted? We both know that's not true. You got indifference. I got nothing but disappointed looks and clicking tongues. Unless somehow I managed to live up to whatever the fuck their expectations were. Do you have any idea how difficult that was?"

I sighed softly and leaned against Riley. "I guess not. But I would have taken that disappointment over them not giving a shit."

"Really?" he asked, disbelieving. "You would have gone to law school because they forced you to? No you wouldn't. You liked being able to screw around with your sculptures. Boo fucking hoo when you couldn't stand up for hours and make them any more. You could still paint, draw or whatever art you want to do. I don't see them up here, dragging you home to make them into whatever puppet they want."

"I don't see them dragging you back either," I said quietly.

Did he really need to throw my arthritis in my face every chance he got? It shattered my dreams and turned my life upside down. Yes, I could still paint and draw, but they weren't my first loves. My sculptures were everything to me until I couldn't make them any more. Now, that part of me felt hollow. Ironic, given where we were.

"I'm not going back," Brooks said. He leaned back in his chair and slumped as though defeated. He sat that way for a moment or two before rallying and sitting up straight again. Typical of him; he never let anything get him down for long. Even if taking a moment to wallow was healthy.

"I know you hated university," I said. "You always seemed miserable, but I didn't think you wanted my..."

"Pity? No I didn't. I don't now. I fucking hated every minute of it. It felt like a prison sentence." His mouth twisted.

"What do you want to do with the rest of your life?" Riley asked. He seemed sympathetic, but not pitying. Ready to be a sounding board if Brooks wanted one.

"I don't fucking know," Brooks said, ending the sentence on a sigh. He glanced over at me before pushing his chair back and hurrying away, the door shutting behind him.

"He seems nice," Riley said with a touch of sarcasm. "No offence, but your parents seem like assholes."

I laughed softly. "They have their moments." I was starting to see that more and more. I always thought Brooks was the golden child, but now I thought about it, he was the one who was held up as a model to me. He was right, he was expected to do everything perfectly, and conform to whatever they wanted him to be. He grew up under the weight of their expectations. I supposed I was lucky I didn't. The disinterest sucked, but the pressure would have been heavy as hell.

"I wish we talked about this sooner," I said, looking back at the closed door. "We could have helped each other." Instead, we'd gone through it more or less alone. Resenting each other while we could have cried on each other's shoulders. Or more.

"Just guessing, but he doesn't seem like the chatty type," Riley said. "I don't think opening up to you, or anyone, was something he planned on doing. He must have had enough for it to come out now."

I swore under my breath. "You're right. I didn't even think to ask if anything had happened."

"He didn't give you a chance," Connor said. "If he wants to open up, he will."

"What Connor said," Riley agreed. "In my lifetime of experience with temperamental assholes, give him time to cool down."

Connor cut him a look. "Lifetime of being one too."

"Also that," Riley agreed. "I'm not as temperamental as you or him. Or Josiah, for that matter. He puts the mood in moody."

"Can you blame him?" I asked. "I'd be moody too if everyone treated me the way they treated him."

Riley took my hand. "It sounds to me like that's exactly what happened. You were both treated like outsiders. Like you weren't wanted. Josiah's was, I don't know, on a bigger scale, but it amounts to the same thing. People were shitty to you and to him. You didn't deserve that."

"Neither did he," I said, giving Riley a watery smile. "Neither did Brooks. I'm starting to think I should set up a support group instead of a gallery. Basket Cases Anonymous."

"That doesn't sound very anonymous," Riley said. "But if you do that, can I come? I have plenty of issues myself."

"Like what?" Connor looked at him doubtfully.

"I'm painfully shy," Riley said, pretending to look innocent.

"You're full of shit," Connor told him.

Riley pointed a finger at him. "That, right there. I'm scarred for life."

Connor rolled his eyes and shook his head. "Anyway, Riley and I were talking."

"Okay," I said slowly. "Should I be worried? All of the administration for work is up to date." I didn't think this was about me working for them.

"Shame, I would have liked to punish you with my hand on your ass," Connor said. "No, we were talking about you doing a DNA test."

I blinked a couple of times. It took a few moments for my brain to catch up with what he was saying and the implications.

"I thought you said it wasn't possible for me to be…" I lowered my voice. "Coral Clarke."

"I'm not sure it is." He creased his brow. "But we could rule it out."

"I suppose it couldn't hurt," I said after a couple of

moments. "But don't we need to get DNA from Gavin?"

"That'll be the hard bit," Connor said. "Maybe you can talk to my sister or Fiona? See if one of them will talk to him."

"You think it's a good idea to involve more people in this?" I looked from him to Riley and back again.

"Those two won't tell anyone," Connor said. "It shouldn't go any further than that. We don't need to feed the town's fucking grapevine. They'll figure out something weird is up soon enough." He didn't seem happy about that, but there wasn't much we could do when it came to small town gossip.

"I'll talk to Fiona over lunch," I said. "She seems to have a way of getting him to open up." This whole thing is going to be a delicate operation. If it was for nothing, it could be even more damaging to him than the past was. Digging up old skeletons never ended well.

"Speaking of lunch, we should grab some and get back to work," Connor said. "We have to get the skis and snowboards ready for when the snow is heavier."

Riley rubbed his hands together. "I can't fucking wait. The best time of year ever." His smile faded. "I guess you can't... Ski?" He looked like he was worried he'd stuck his foot in his mouth, complete with a huge snow boot. Maybe even a ski.

"I can sit in a sled," I said. "And I can make a mean snowman. Don't even get me started on my snowball throwing arm." I raised it and pretended to warm up for a big swing.

Okay, I wasn't that good at throwing snowballs, but I wasn't going to dampen his enthusiasm for the height of winter. That was when their business brought the most customers up to Aurora Hollow. For seven days a week, they'd be busy teaching people to ski and snowboard, and getting them around the slopes. From what I gathered, there was a ski lift belonging to Aurora Lodge. I hadn't seen it when I was up there, but I had other things on my mind at the time. I was looking forward to riding on it, and enjoying the view as well as the activities. And any moment I got to spend with them in their busiest season.

He brightened up again. "Now I really can't wait. If you see me moving funny, I'm doing a snow dance." He swayed in his chair.

"Stop that." Connor grimaced at him. "People are going to think you're weird."

"They don't already?" I teased.

"Weird*er*," Connor conceded.

"Sorry, I'm all out of fucks," Riley said, his eyes half closed.

"I'm starting to think he's the one we should throw off the lookout," Connor grumbled. "Come on, dickhead, we have work to do." He stood and brushed his lips over mine before heading to the pub's small kitchen to get something to eat.

10

───────

LEAH

"I swear, I forget how cold it gets." Fiona laughed and slipped out of her coat. She draped it over the back of a chair and sat, rubbing her reddened hands together. "Why does something so pretty have to be so cold? Snow, I mean."

I joined in her laughter. "I figured that was what you meant. I don't know. I guess if it wasn't so cold, it would be raining."

She wrinkled her nose. "Right, rain is much worse than cold. So, how have you been?"

I let out a long breath and told her about Brooks turning up in town. I didn't mention him watching me. That would definitely be heading into TMI territory.

"Did he bring any friends with him?" She gave me a sly smile.

"Not that I know of, but if he did I'll be sure to give them your number," I said. Although, she could do better than any of his friends.

"You're so sweet." She patted my hand. "You look like something else is on your mind." She looked expectantly at me, her mouth pulled over to one side.

"You could say that," I said. "We should order—" I was interrupted by Connor placing plates in front of us. Each with a burger and a side of fries.

"Compliments of the owner," he said in a grunt. Before either of us could say thank you, he disappeared into the back of the pub.

"There's advantages to knowing the boss." Fiona picked up a fry and popped it into her mouth. "Mmm, so good."

"Connor said something about them having a new cook, so we might be guinea pigs." That didn't stop me from picking up my burger and taking a bite. I decided she was right, it was good. Juicy and tender without being greasy.

"If this is what we get as an experiment, sign me up," she said happily. "So, you were saying?" Clearly she wasn't letting me off that easy.

"This is going to sound wild," I warned her.

"I feel like at this point you've been in Aurora Hollow for long enough to know I've pretty much heard everything." She bit into another fry and gave me an 'out with it' gesture with her hand.

"Okay, but keep an open mind," I said. I quickly explained how I'd taken the nails up to Josiah, and he'd shown me around. The longer I talked, the wider her eyes got.

"Holy shit," she whispered. "That would explain a bunch of things. Why I immediately felt comfortable with you. I didn't even hesitate to offer you the keys to the cottage beside mine, because I trusted you. It all makes sense now. We were kids together for a while."

My brow scrunched so hard it hurt. "You believe me? You think it's possible I could be...her?" The people at the next table weren't listening, but just in case, it seemed like a good idea not to say the name Coral Clarke out loud.

"I don't see why not," Fiona said thoughtfully. "I mean, it backs up what Josiah said all those years ago. It raises a bunch of other questions, but it answers some. And you want me to help you to find out the truth?"

"It's the only way to know for sure," I said.

"Maybe I'm wrong and I'm losing my mind, but maybe I'm right. If nothing else, I think I deserve to know."

"I'm not saying you're wrong," she said slowly. "But think about the implications if you're right. What does that mean for you and your family?"

I shook my head. "I have no idea."

"Do you really want to turn everything upside down?" she asked, still being as gentle as she could. "You might dig out skeletons you don't want to deal with."

"I know," I said on a sigh. "But Gavin and Josiah deserve the truth."

"You really care about him, don't you?" she asked. "Josiah, I mean. I see it in your eyes when you say his name. What do Riley and Connor think about that?"

"They're prepared to deal with whatever situation we find ourselves in," I said carefully.

"They don't mind if you have another boyfriend?" She seemed impressed. "Can I be you when I grow up?"

I snorted. "You don't want to be me. But there's no reason you can't have what I have. You need to meet the right guys."

"Which brings me back to your stepbrother and his friends." She grinned. "But seriously, I can help you with Gavin. We'll need to figure out what we're going to tell him. Maybe we could suggest it's a health check."

"I don't like lying to him." I grimaced. But when came down to it, I didn't see any other way. We couldn't come out and tell him the whole truth. Not without risking his mental health any further.

"I think you could say it's in a good cause," she said. "The hospital here is small, but it might have the swabs we'd need to do a test. I have a friend who works there, we can ask her. She'll be discreet. Trust me, it isn't the first time anyone in town needed a DNA test done. Things happen over the long, cold winter." She made a 'you know how people get' face.

"I'm sure they do," I said with a short laugh. "Okay, I think we should do it. Thank you, I owe you one."

"It's nothing," she said lightly. "This whole thing has hung over Aurora Hollow for the last twenty years. It'd be nice if it could be put to rest."

"With any luck, we can do that," I said. She was right though, it was going to open a big can of worms over the last twenty years of my life. Questions about my mother I wasn't sure I wanted to know the answers to. Questions I'd get to when the time came.

I might be wrong about all of this. If that was the case, it would be better if my mother didn't know I was poking my nose into it. Brooks couldn't know either. I couldn't trust he wouldn't go to her, either to confront her or fill her in. No, he'd know when the time was right.

"When do you want to do this?" Fiona asked.

"The sooner the better," I said. "It's going to take time for the test results to come back." I wasn't sure if I was going to be able to sleep while waiting for them. I'd have to, because chances were it'd take weeks. I have to get on with my life in the meantime.

"Okay, I'll talk to Jenny after work. Maybe we could go and see Gavin tomorrow morning before work? Get him after he's had a good night sleep. He might be more amenable then." She seemed to have it all figured out.

"That sounds like a plan to me," I said. "I really can't thank you enough." Honestly, I'd half expected her to laugh and dismiss all of this as some sort of crazy hallucination. Why wouldn't she? It certainly sounded off the wall.

"No need to thank me," she said. "I'm honoured you trust me enough to come to me with this. It means a lot." She gave me a sincere smile. Not for a moment wavering from her belief in me. I couldn't remember the last time anyone had faith like that. She wasn't even stopping to question my sanity. I'd add 'yet,' but I didn't think she was going to. Even if this was nuts, she was here for the ride.

"I do trust you," I said with equal sincerity. "You've been nothing but sweet to me since I arrived in town. If it wasn't for you, I might not have stuck around."

"I'm sure you would have," she said. "But that's nice of you to say. I really did feel connected to you from that first conversation in the Snowdrop Café. You belong here. If anyone still disagrees with that, I'll throw hands." She grinned and raised them, as if ready to swing a punch. A couple of silver rings glittered on her fingers. If she punched anyone with those, it would hurt.

"I believe you would," I said with a laugh. "Although, I think you might have to get in line behind Connor and Riley." And maybe Josiah. Not to mention Whitney and Holly. The fact the list was even that long was gratifying.

"I'll throw hands with Connor and Riley over who throws hands against anyone who says you don't belong here." She frowned, as if trying to figure out that made sense, before nodding. "They wouldn't dare to take me on."

"Of course not, you're terrifying." I ate my last fry and wiped my hands on a napkin. "I'm surprised they don't run away every time you step into the room."

"Right?" She laughed again. "Me too. They must be tougher than I thought they were."

"It just goes to show you, you can know someone for a long time and still be surprised," I teased.

She smiled at that, but it faded. "You know what? I'm going to be sad, in a way, if it turns out to be true." She was also careful not to mention Coral Clarke. "We will have missed out on so many years of hanging out together. Giggling over stupid shit and doing each other's make-up. Think about all that shit disturbing we could have done, with Riley and Connor."

I had a feeling she'd done enough of that for both of us. Her expression and line of thought were contagious. My mood was a little heavier as I contemplated.

What would growing up with them have been like? Would I think of them as brothers, the way she did? That would certainly change things. I might have the same relationship with them that Fiona, Whitney and Holly did. Nothing more than friends. And Josiah? He might have just been another one of the guys in town. Not treated like trash. I never would have met Brooks.

"We can still hang out, do make-up and give them shit," I said. "If it is true… I'm here now."

"Yes, you are." She put a hand on my bicep and squeezed gently. "We can make up for all that lost time."

"If the time was lost," I reminded her. "And if it wasn't, then we can still do all those things. Regardless of where I came from, I'm still me. Still Leah Kent."

"The one and only." She wiped her fingers on her napkin and tossed it onto her plate. "Unfortunately, I have to get back to work."

"So do I," I said. I was going to try to rebuild the adventure tours website, to make it a little more user-friendly. Riley did a good job building it, but it could be tweaked here and there to improve it.

"I'll see you in the morning then." We both stood and she gave me a hug. "Tell Connor I said thanks for lunch. I'll eat here more often if he's going to feed us like that."

"If I ate like that too many times, you'd have to roll me out the door." I patted my stomach. It was nice, once in a while, but if I kept going like this, I was going to have to find the hot springs or an indoor, heated pool to work it all off. I used to run and ride my bike, but these days it was all about water. Good exercise and gentle on my limbs.

"Me too." Fiona snagged her coat and shoved her arms into it. While I returned the plates to the bar, she hurried out the door.

11

RILEY

"Looks like we got off light." I inspected the last of our snowboards and leaned it up with the rest. "We were lucky. Only a couple need repair."

"It's not luck. We take care of our stuff." Connor glanced at me as if I shouldn't forget that. Like he'd let me. "Saves us a ton of money in the long run. And hassle."

"Are we still talking about snowboards?" I asked. I picked up a snow boot and started to look it over carefully, before putting it aside with the snowboards. "Or are we talking about Leah?"

"All of the above," Connor said. "I want to have a conversation with that Brooks asshole. He seems to have a chip on his shoulder bigger than mine."

That was saying something. Chip was Connor's

middle name. Literally, his middle name was Charles. Which, when you thought about it, was pretty funny.

"I noticed that about him." I inspected another boot and put it beside the first. "He seems high maintenance." Smoking hot, but a lot of work. Like Leah, but she didn't walk around like she thought the world owed her anything. Brooks seemed to think the world owed him *everything*. Yeah, apparently I had a type.

Connor snorted. "That's one word for it. I'm half tempted to put him on a toboggan and drop him off at the top of a slope. The kind that ends in a cliff." His eyes glazed for a moment, like he was picturing Brooks' rapid descent, flying off the end into the abyss and disappearing.

"I thought that's what you meant," I said. My phone buzzed in my back pocket. I pulled it out and glanced at the screen. "Speak of the devil. Holly said he's staying at the Snowbank Hotel. Room twenty-one."

"Do I want to know how Holly knows that?" Connor handed me another pair of boots to put in the pile that didn't need repairs.

"Probably not." I sent off a thanks to her and put

my phone back. "For what it's worth, I don't think she's fucking Brooks."

Connor shrugged. "It'd make life easier if she was. Then he wouldn't want to get his dick wet in Leah."

"Yeah, he definitely wants to do that." The way he looked at her, like he wanted to tear off her clothes and bury himself deep inside her. Who could blame him? She had the most perfect pussy. And mouth. And...everything else. I had no problem admitting I was head over heels for the woman. I was gone from the moment I saw her sitting in front of her easel. Absently, I rubbed my nose where I'd gotten paint on it from 'accidentally' getting too close. I'd wanted to see her reaction and she hadn't disappointed me.

I also hadn't missed the fact neither she nor Connor said they loved me when I told them, but that was okay. I knew how they felt. They'd say it soon enough.

"I think we're done here for the day." He straightened up, his hands in the back pockets of his jeans. "Let's go and talk to this dickhead."

"Are you going to punch him?" I shoved Connor out the door and closed the storage shed behind us before locking it carefully.

"Only if it becomes necessary," Connor said. "Wouldn't want to damage his pretty little nose."

"You think his nose is pretty?" I pocketed the keys and followed Connor out to the road.

Connor punched my bicep. "Not as pretty as yours, asshole. Stop fishing for compliments."

I rubbed my bicep and grinned. "I wasn't fishing, just asking a question." I was totally fishing. I wasn't jealous of Brooks or any feelings Leah or Connor might have toward him, but I wanted to know where they stood with him. If the vibe I was getting was right. It seemed to me like everyone wanted everyone else. After we cleared a bunch of air.

Connor rolled his eyes at me. "I know you better than that. You practically had your rod in your hand, bait on the hook."

"And now you're thinking about having my rod in your hand." I grinned. I could almost feel his calloused fingers wrapped around me, stroking slowly, coaxing me toward orgasm. His eyes dark while he watched me draw closer and closer to the edge. Me decorating his hand with my cum.

He rammed his shoulder into mine without slowing the pace. "Later. We need to deal with this guy first."

"And by deal with him, you mean..." I teased. Connor was the one who brought the word rod into the conversation. If he didn't want me aroused, he shouldn't have gone there. Even if he did it unintentionally, the result was the same.

"I'm not going there to fuck him," Connor said bluntly. "We owe it to Leah to know what his agenda is. He didn't follow her all the way here for nothing. And I don't think he followed her here so he could fuck her either. A guy like that, he could get pussy whenever he wanted. No, there's more to it than that."

"Guys have done less for a certain pussy," I pointed out. "And he saw hers who knows how many times? I've seen it less often and I'm addicted." Honestly, I was addicted to hers before I saw it, because of the way Connor described her to me. The reality was even better.

"Imagine seeing her pussy and never touching it." If anything was going to drive me crazy in life, it would be that. Never being able to touch her and make her come… No wonder Brooks was so uptight. I would be too, in his situation.

"Nightmare material," Connor said.

"Exactly."

We walked the couple of blocks to the small hotel on the edge of town. Little more than a handful of rooms over two levels, and a reception office, it was one of the cheaper places to stay in Aurora Hollow.

From this time of year on, it'd be booked solid. Brooks must have been lucky to get a room here at all.

I followed Connor carefully up the steps to the second floor, and over the landing to room twenty-one. He hammered on the door and we both stood outside and waited.

After a minute or two, the door swung inwards and Brooks stood inside, glaring at us.

"Oh look, it's the dickhead twins," he said sarcastically. "What the fuck do you want?"

Connor shouldered him out of the way and stepped inside. "To talk."

I smiled at Brooks before stepping past him, into the tiny room.

A queen size bed took up most of the space, the covers faded, but cosy. Another door led to a small, neat bathroom. A bright green suitcase sat against a wall, the lid open. The contents were neatly folded inside several packing cubes, which were also open. The guy hadn't packed in a hurry. And he took his time to carefully repack. Fair enough, this room would get overrun with stuff in a blink if he let it.

Brooks sighed and closed the door, keeping the warmth in. "What do you want to talk about? The weather? Wait, let me guess. You want to compare cock sizes."

"I mean…" I raised my eyebrows at both of them. "What? A guy gets curious." My gaze dropped to their groins speculatively. If I had to guess, I'd say they were both as big as each other. Nice. I bet Brooks knew what to do with his too. Connor sure did.

So did I, of course.

"We're not here to compare cock size." Connor slid me a look. "I'd win anyway. We're here to talk about Leah."

"No shit." Brooks leaned his back against the door and crossed his arms. "If you've come to tell me to stay away from her—"

"We haven't," Connor said. "That's up to her."

"Then why are you here?" Brooks closed his eyes as if that might make us disappear. Good luck with that, since he was blocking the only exit.

"We want to know why you followed her here," I said bluntly, since they were only going to beat around the bush anyway. "You seem angry with her because your parents were assholes." Was Leah actually related to any of them? Not Brooks, obviously, not his father. What about her mother? This whole situation was complicated. And yet, at the same time it wasn't. She was still Leah, when it came down to it. Still the woman I loved. The woman Connor loved.

"She's impulsive," Brooks said. "She took off up here and I wanted to know why. What's the big deal about Aurora Hollow?" He jerked his head back toward the door, making a blonde curl fall over one eye. He shoved it back impatiently.

"Hello? Have you looked around town?" I cocked my head at him. "This place is special."

Brooks scoffed. "I don't see what's so special about it. It's fucking snowing outside."

"Congratulations, hammer, on hitting the nail right on the head." I smirked. "That's just one of the things that makes it special. So you came here because you were curious about where Leah was living?"

"I don't buy it," Connor said. "If you resent her so much, why would you give a shit about where she is?" He tucked his hands into his pockets again and leaned back. His hazel eyes were intense, wanting the whole truth, or at least some blunt honesty. As much as Brooks was willing to give right now.

Brooks narrowed his eyes at him. "I don't resent her. I fucking hate them. I hate what they did to both of us. But her..." He shook his head slowly.

"You're in love with her," I blurted. "You were watching her, and you followed her because you love her. But you're sure she doesn't feel the same way."

He slid me a resentful glance. "Why should she? I've always been an asshole to her."

I shared a silent look with Connor. "Maybe this is your chance to *not* be an asshole to her."

"What are you talking about?" Brooks pushed himself off the door.

"Leah has gone through a lot," I said. "I was thinking of doing something nice for her tonight. Something romantic. If you agree not to be a dick-head, maybe we'll invite you to come along."

I'd taken Connor by surprise with that, but he rallied quickly and nodded. "She deserves to be spoilt. We're the guys to do it." His expression was challenging, as if he was suggesting Brooks wasn't up to it. Of course in doing that, he knew the other guy wouldn't have a choice. If only to prove Connor wrong, Brooks would go along with it.

I didn't miss the way the front of Connor's jeans was tighter. We would spoil her like that too, but I had something else in mind first.

I briefly thought about Josiah, but tonight was not the night to try to make amends with him. We'd have to figure that out soon though. If he'd even let us. If I was him, I'd probably tell us to fuck all the way off. For Leah's sake, we'd have to try. If he wanted nothing to do with us, we'd figure that out later too. One step at a time.

"What sort of spoiling?" Brooks still looked doubtful, but curious in spite of himself. He knew he was being played, but for now we had an understanding. How long would it last? That was anyone's guess. Hopefully long enough for my fantasies to come to life.

"Well…" I started.

12

LEAH

I WAS ALMOST FINISHED UPDATING the website when the door opened. I hadn't bothered to lock it. What was the point when the guys already had a key?

I closed the laptop and looked up to see Connor and Riley step inside, followed by Brooks. He looked at me like this was the last place on earth he wanted to step foot into. He still took a good look around, as if assessing where a camera could go.

"What are you all doing here?" I asked. Especially together. That was unexpected and interesting. So far, no one looked punched, or coerced.

"We brought you a few things." Riley and Connor placed bags down on the table before Riley headed into the kitchen..

"Hope you're hungry." Connor opened one bag

and started to pull out plastic boxes, the inside coated with steam that obscured the contents. He cracked each one and poured pasta into the bowls Riley brought over.

"I am now." I inhaled the delicious smell of tomato, truffles and meatballs mixed with spaghetti. "That smells amazing."

From another bag, Connor pulled a bottle of wine. He set it down on the table before dipping his hand back into the bag and coming out with a bunch of wildflowers.

"They're so pretty." I hurried over to the mantelpiece to pick up a vase and carry it over to the table.

"Friend of ours has a greenhouse," Connor said. "Mostly for vegetables, but he has some flowers too." He looked like he thought that was a waste of greenhouse space, but he still slid them into the vase and placed them in the centre of the table.

"This is so thoughtful of you." I managed to find four wine glasses that more or less matched and placed them in front of our bowls.

"It was Riley's idea," Brooks said. He picked up an unopened bag and placed it aside, suggesting whatever was in there was for later.

"They helped," Riley said as he slipped into a chair. "Connor makes a mean pasta sauce."

Connor shrugged. "A long time ago, I thought I'd be a chef."

"What happened?" I settled into my chair and picked up my fork.

"I decided being stuck inside all day would suck, and I like eating better." Connor opened the wine and poured us all a glass each.

"I'll drink to that." Riley grinned and raised his glass.

"Being inside isn't so bad," Brooks muttered, but he joined in the toast before downing a gulp of wine.

"Brooks doesn't like the snow," Riley said, looking amused.

"It's fucking cold," Brooks said. "Couldn't you run off to somewhere warm? I hear San Diego is nice this time of year. Or the Bahamas. Maybe Melbourne."

"I like it here," I said. "I hate heat and humidity." Feeling sweaty and sticky wasn't pleasant. Not unless orgasms were involved.

"I'd melt in a place like that," Riley said. "My mother says I'm part snowman."

"Which part?" Brooks asked. "Do you have a carrot for a dick?"

Riley laughed. "No. Mine tastes much better."

Brooks' face turned slightly pink. "That wouldn't be hard, carrot tastes disgusting."

"It would definitely be hard." Riley waggled his eyebrows. "As a matter of fact—"

"Let's finish eating first," Connor said. "Leah is going to need her strength."

I paused with a meatball halfway to my mouth. "Am I now?" Okay, I knew they weren't here just to bring me food and flowers. Which made me even more curious about Brooks' inclusion. I knew what he wanted and I wanted it too, but there was the question of their willingness to share. Or was there? Possibly not, given they'd brought him with them.

"Definitely," Connor said. Neither of the other two disagreed with him.

"I hope you brought dessert then," I said.

"We might have." Riley gave a cagey glance toward the last bag. "You'll have to wait and see."

"Be a good girl and finish your dinner," Connor said.

My panties were officially ruined.

Brooks regarded me, his blue eyes intense, curious. I could almost hear him thinking, processing my response to Connor's praise. Wondering if it stemmed from my lack of parental attention, or if I just liked it. I may never know for sure myself.

Either way, he was understanding this new thing about me. And now I wondered if he felt the same.

I chewed over that for a moment, but suspected he preferred the opposite. He was so used to being told he was good for jumping through hoops. I bet there was a rebellious side in there. One that was itching to be let out.

"This is so good," I said, washing a meatball down with wine. "You would have been a great chef."

"I'm a better adventure tour operator," Connor said gruffly.

"I second that," Riley said.

"Your parents are good with that?" Brooks asked. "Skiing and snowboarding for a living?"

Connor bristled. For a moment I thought he might snap at Brooks. Maybe aim his fork at his eye…

I put a hand on his bicep, encouraging him to take a moment and think before he responded.

"My dad wants me to take over the Frosty Brew," Connor said finally. "I don't want to. It's not where my heart is." He slid Brooks a gaze as if daring him to contradict him.

Riley looked from him to Brooks and back again and said, "Bro."

Connor squinted at him. "Bro?"

Riley nodded. "Bro." As if the exchange made any sort of sense at all.

"They must get drunk easily," Brooks remarked.

I swallowed down a laugh. "Maybe you guys can speak in English. Try a full sentence or two."

"Connor wants to hire a manager to run the pub," Riley said, looking excited. "I'm guessing Brooks needs a job."

His words were followed by silence as everyone wrapped their heads around that suggestion.

"You want me to run a pub?" Brooks looked disbelieving.

"Why not?" It was me who answered. "You're smart. You know how to handle people. The pub is indoors. Well, most of it. Why couldn't you manage it? If you're planning to stay in town, that is?"

"I hate to say it, but Riley is right," Connor said. "If my dad agrees and you want the job, I can stick around until you're trained. You'll be working for my father, and for me, but you'd have a lot of leeway. And Riley and I could focus on our business."

Brooks shook his head, looking bewildered. "I mean, I guess I could give it a try. It's gotta be better than law."

"You don't even have to wear a suit," Riley said.

"But you could, if you wanted to," I said, half-teasing. People in town would think it was an interesting look, but I doubted it would catch on.

"Fuck that," Brooks said with a snort. "I'll throw all my suits on the fire. I'll keep a few ties though. They might come in useful." He looked over at me meaningfully.

"If I wasn't hard already," Riley said half under his breath.

Connor hummed his agreement.

"Is this where someone suggests we let dinner go down before we have dessert?" I asked. My stepfather would have insisted on waiting between courses. Because only crass people hurried through meals or some shit. Me, I was just there to eat.

"I don't see why we should wait," Riley said. He threw back the rest of his wine and stood, grabbing up bowls and taking them to the kitchen.

Connor and Brooks stood to either side of me and offered me a hand.

I looked from one to the other before accepting both of them and letting them guide me out from behind the table. Without a word, they took me into my bedroom and started to peel off my clothes. Riley hurried in to join, throwing my discarded garments into a pile to the side of the room.

"Is this what you've been watching?" Connor

asked Brooks. He trailed the tip of one finger from my lips, down my collarbone and over the curve of my breast. "Watching without touching?"

"Yeah," Brooks said breathlessly. "So fucking perfect."

"So fucking ours," Riley added in a whisper.

"Such a good girl, letting us look at you like this." Connor traced a lazy circle around my nipple before sliding his finger back up to my chin. He lifted it and brushed his lips over mine before turning my face toward Riley. Riley kissed me softly and slowly, then leaned back so Connor could turn my face toward Brooks.

"Are you sure about this?" Brooks whispered.

"Very sure," I replied.

He locked his eyes on me. "Good girl." He pressed his mouth to mine, his tongue sliding between my lips to taste the inside of my mouth.

"You're not good, are you Brooks?" Connor asked. "You don't want to be good. You want to fuck your stepsister because you think it's wrong."

"So fucking wrong," Brooks whispered. "I need to taste her."

Between them, they lay me back on the bed. Riley slipped out to grab the last bag. He carried it back into the bedroom, opened it and pulled out a bottle of chocolate sauce. Smiling, he cracked open the lid and started to trickle the cool, sweet sauce over my breasts, down my belly and over the insides of my thighs.

"I might have forgotten to mention, you're dessert." He sat beside me and trickled some of the sauce into my mouth.

I caught a few drops and swallowed. "Mmm, that's good."

"It's even tastier here." Riley put the bottle down and started to lick sauce from my nipples.

A jolt of heat shot straight to my core, leaving me panting for more.

Brooks, his eyes dark, lowered himself to his stomach and parted my thighs with his hands. He licked up one thigh, cleaning the sauce away before working on the other, inching his way closer to my pussy. Finally, he looked me in the eye and tasted my pussy with the tip of his tongue.

"Fuck, you taste better than chocolate." He started licking and nibbling slowly, his finger working its way inside me. Then another.

"I bet I taste good with chocolate." Riley shred his clothes and trickled chocolate onto his cock before kneeling beside me and pressing his head against my lips. "Be a good girl; open up and tell me."

I opened my mouth, taking his cock all the way down to the back of my throat. His skin was a combination of sweet from the chocolate and salty from his pre-cum. I hummed my approval at the flavour. If I could bottle this, I'd be rich.

Connor stripped off and sat on the other side of me, licking the rest of the chocolate from my nipples, grazing his teeth over the stiff peaks.

With Riley tapping the back of my throat and the other two working me so expertly, I couldn't help coming in only a handful of moments. Shattering into an oblivion filled with a million stars before slowly coming back together. Riley pulled out of me to let me catch my breath.

Brooks kissed his way down my thighs while pulling his clothes off and throwing them aside. "I need to be inside you."

Connor looked over at him. "You can do better than that."

Brooks opened his mouth as if he was about to tell him to fuck off, but then he nodded. "Leah, you're going to be a good fucking girl and let your stepbrother fuck you."

He crawled up the bed until he was lying over me. "It's so fucking wrong to want to be inside my stepsister, but I don't care. I'm going to fuck you. I'm going to come inside you. I'm going to fill my step-sister with my cum."

"Much better." Connor nodded approvingly.

Brooks rolled his eyes, but pushed my legs apart with his knees. "Be a good girl and tell me you want me."

"I want you," I said, my voice barely above a whisper. "I want to be a good girl and let my stepbrother fuck me."

Those words must have pushed him over the edge, because he lined himself up and rammed himself into me all the way to the hilt.

"Fuck," he groaned. "You feel better than I imagined. So fucking tight. So fucking mine."

Connor cleared his throat.

"So fucking *ours*," Brooks corrected.

"Exactly." Riley pressed his cock back between my lips. "So fucking ours."

Giving Brooks a quick glance, Connor worked his fingers between him and me to push his thumb down to my clit. Almost sending me over the edge again.

Brooks eyes rolled back in his head as he thrust, the base of his cock sliding against Connor's hand each time. "That feels... Fuck."

"So good," Riley finished for him. He thrust a

little faster between my lips, his eyes half closed as he did right before he came. His orgasm took him a moment later, washing him away and forcing his release to flood my mouth.

I managed to hold it until he'd milked every drop and slid out of me. With a curl of my fingers, I urged Connor over to me. He pressed his mouth to mine, letting me push Riley's cum into his mouth.

"Such a good, dirty girl," Riley said approvingly.

Connor raised his eyebrows and swallowed. "Delicious." He licked his lips.

"You guys…" Brooks grunted and came, grinding against me, crying out his own release to the ceiling. Filling me the way he'd promised he would. "So incredible." He sagged down over me, panting for a moment before rolling off and letting Connor take his place.

Connor rolled me over onto my side, facing him. He carefully draped one of my legs over his and pressed into my wet, leaking pussy. He looked from Riley to Brooks and back again.

"I can't decide whose cum feels better inside her. I think it's a tie." He shrugged and started to thrust slowly. Taking his time and making sure he wasn't hurting me with his deep, hard strokes.

"She's worth the wait, isn't she?" Riley said softly to Brooks.

"Worth every minute of it," Brooks agreed, his eyes focused on me like he was trying to memorise every moment. No one had bothered to get a phone to film any of this, which I didn't mind a bit. It was nice to be in the moment with all three of them.

I really thought that? All three of them? I was here in my little cottage in the mountains, fucking three smoking hot, incredible men. I could hardly believe it was real, but I didn't want to wake up if it wasn't.

Best. Fantasy. Ever.

Connor groaned and then he was thrusting faster, more deliberately before he lost himself in his own orgasm, spilling himself inside me and filling me up further. His face was pink, his hazel eyes glazed with concentration and pleasure. And then he was sagging and pulling me to him.

"So perfect," he whispered. "Our good girl."

In the corner of my eye, I saw Riley nudge Brooks with his elbow. "Welcome to the family."

13

LEAH

"Are you sure about this?" Fiona stopped in front of Gavin's front door, her hand raised. "Once we do this, it's done. Whatever the result is, there's no going back."

In her other hand, she held a bag containing two swabs. One for me and one for him. It all looked so harmless, and yet it could put a bomb under everything and everyone I'd ever known. The fallout could be catastrophic, but I didn't see a choice. I didn't want to spend the rest of my life wondering, selfish though I knew that was.

I sucked in a breath, held it for a moment and let it back out.

"I'm sure," I said finally. For a moment, I wished one of my guys was with me. Connor and Riley were with a group zip lining, and Brooks was in the pub, learning the basics. Jacob Ferguson agreed to take him on, but he'd have to start from the bottom. Working behind the bar, serving customers and wiping tables.

I'd half-expected Brooks to object, but he hadn't seemed to mind. For now. Honestly, I couldn't remember a time when I saw him as relaxed as he was after last night. As if fucking me took the weight of the world off his shoulders. And the pressure out of his balls. I'd run his dirty talk through my mind over and over again, my pulse ratcheting up each time. We weren't related and we didn't grown up together, but if it got him going I'd take every word of it. And give it back in equal measure.

Fiona nodded and knocked on the door before turning the knob to open it. "Gavin? Are you decent?"

Hopefully he was, because she marched on in. If he wasn't, I suspected she wouldn't be too concerned. After all, she'd taken care of one human being, what was another here or there? Although, there was a big difference between a little girl and an adult male. Especially when she was related to one of them and not the other.

Holding back a laugh, I followed her inside,

closing the door behind me. The inside of the house was immediately warmer, the cold left behind out on the street.

"Morning." Gavin was sitting in the same chair as the last time I was here. This time, he was finishing off a plate of toast and what smelled like a cup of tea. A fire was burning happily in the wood stove to the side of the room. It was small, but it kept the place cosy. A pile of logs sat beside it, ready to be tossed in to keep the flames fed.

"Oh good, you're eating," Fiona said. "You're looking well." She placed the packets on the table and her hands on her hips.

"Fighting fit," he said with a grunt. "Louisa is doing my laundry."

"I'm not here about your laundry," Fiona said. "Just a quick check up. I'm going to need you to finish your tea and brush your teeth."

"Are you my mother?" But Gavin picked up his tea and drank down the rest of it.

"Lucky for both of us, no." Fiona laughed. "Just looking out for you."

"You're not the nurse," Gavin observed.

"You're very sharp today." Fiona picked up his plate and cup and took them into the kitchen. "I haven't seen you so sassy in a long time."

Gavin grunted. "You're the sassy one, girl." He gripped the arms of his chair and levered himself to his feet. "What am I doing?" He glanced around. Started to sit back down.

Fiona grabbed his shoulders before he could. "Your teeth, Gavin. I need you to brush your teeth. Good dental health is important, remember?" She nodded encouragingly a few times and with a little bit too much enthusiasm, but he didn't seem to realise how cagey she was behaving. Or he did and he let it slide.

Gavin muttered something, but shuffled off to the bathroom to brush his teeth before returning and flopping back down into his chair. He got himself settled and frowned at us.

"What are you doing here?"

Fiona glanced at me and grimaced. "This won't take a moment. We just need you to open your mouth so I can put this inside." She picked up a swab and tore the packet open. "I just need to swipe the inside of your cheek and then we're done."

She made it sound easy, but Gavin eyed her like she was out of her mind.

"It really is that simple," I said, hoping to reassure him. Also really hoping to get out of here before Louisa returned and wondered what the hell we were up to. This would be difficult to explain without telling her more than I was ready for her to know. Not to mention, there might be laws against what we were doing.

"Fiona, maybe you can do mine first. Show him it's painless." I'd have to have my cheek swabbed sooner or later anyway. If it helped to get this over with, then I'd offer myself up, happily.

"Good idea." She stepped over to me and waited for me to open my mouth. Carefully, she swiped the swab up and down the inside of my cheek before pulling it back and dropping it into the bag with my name on it.

"See, nothing to it." She pulled out another and got it ready.

Gavin still gave us both the side eye, but he opened his mouth and let her work quickly before closing it again and flopping back in his chair.

My heart raced as I watched her drop the second swab in the bag with his name on it. Would that give me all the answers I needed? What would I do if it did? I also had to consider the possibility it wouldn't, but that was a bridge I'd deal with when I got to it.

"That was perfect." Fiona closed the Ziploc bag and handed both of them to me. "Thank you so much, Gavin. We'll leave you to it."

He muttered something and nestled down in his chair, looking very much like he was prepared to take a nap. He closed his eyes and a few moments later he was snoring.

I wished I could fall asleep that quickly and easily. Although, after several orgasms the night before, and a bath with the guys' help, I'd slept better than I had in a long time.

I watched him for a few moments, looking for any resemblance between us. Our hair was both brown, but his was mostly grey now. My eyes were blue, his were blue-green. It was possible I resembled my mother. I had no idea what his former wife looked like.

Fiona turned me around and gave me a gentle push towards the door. "I know this is a lot," she whispered.

"What's a lot?" Louisa asked as she stepped through the door, a basket of dry, folded clothes in her arms.

"Making sure Gavin has enough to eat," Fiona said quickly. "I wasn't sure if anyone dropped by today, but I see you have. That's great. I have to get to work." She gave me a quick hug and hurried out, making a quick getaway before Louisa asked her anything else.

Louisa stared after her for a moment, blinked a couple of times and shook her head. "That girl has a good heart, but sometimes she's flighty."

I held back a smile. "Do you need any help?" I gestured toward the laundry basket.

"No, no." She waved me off. "I have everything under control." She placed the basket down on the table. "How's the gallery idea going?"

"I'm still thinking about it," I said honestly. "I like the idea, but it's a big undertaking."

"Anything worth doing usually is," she said. "If you need any help, you only have to ask. You'll have more help than you know what to do with before you can blink."

"I appreciate that, thank you," I said. Everyone told me that from the beginning and they weren't wrong. I couldn't turn around without seeing someone helping someone else, or offering help. Some day, I might even get used to it.

"I better get to work myself," I said.

"How are those boys treating you?" She adjusted her long braid. "Well, I hope."

"Very well," I agreed. "They're good to work for." And even better to play with. Of course, I wasn't going to say that out loud.

"Great." She patted me on the shoulder and

bustled about, putting away Gavin's clothes and washing dishes.

I gave him a last, long look before stepping out into the frigid, morning air. Someone had started to put up decorations for Halloween. Here and there, jack-o'-lanterns and cardboard skeletons hung in the windows. Before long it would be Christmas and we'd be up to our chins in snow. Riley and Connor would be in their element.

I thought about Josiah up there by himself during a blizzard. He must be even lonelier then. Stuck inside his little cottage with only himself for company. If I could, I'd change that for him this year. If he'd let me. Either way, Christmas this year was going to be very different from any I'd had before.

Pulling my coat tighter around myself, I hurried to the post office.

14

LEAH

By mid-afternoon, I hadn't managed to get Josiah off my mind. I wanted to see him, but more than that, I needed to tell him about the DNA test. And the fact more and more people were starting to believe him. I wasn't naïve enough to think it would change anything straight away, but it was a start.

I packed up my laptop and put it away, grabbed my bag and hopped into my car for the winding drive up to his place. Slower than the last time I came up here. The snow hadn't settled, but I watched out for patches of ice. The last thing I needed was to skid off the road and hit a tree.

I finally drove past Aurora Lodge and parked in front of the cottages. He might have been at work at the lodge, but I'd try here first.

As I climbed out of my car, I knew I'd chosen right. A light shone from a small window on the side of what looked like a workshop beside his house.

"Josiah?" I called out, my shoes crunching as I walked across the gravel.

The sound of cursing came from inside right before he stepped out, wiping his hands on his grey track pants.

"What are you doing here?" He leaned against the door frame, dark eyes watching, wary, but predatory. Ready to fight or pounce.

"Just checking up on you," I said lightly. "Things were tense between us last time I was here."

"There is no us." But his eyes lingered on my lips as he spoke. "You shouldn't have wasted your time."

"It's my time, I can use it however I like." I stepped closer, trying to see into the building behind him. Failing, because his body blocked the doorway too well. I had a feeling that was purposeful.

He snort-laughed. "Touché. You're still trespassing on private property."

I cocked my head. "Hmmm, maybe. And maybe one of these cottages belongs to me."

Eyes flashing, he straightened up. "Don't start with that again."

"Starting implies I stopped to begin with," I said. "I haven't. Connor and Riley believe me. Fiona too."

Josiah rubbed a hand over the back of his neck. "Fuck, why did you involve her? Or any of them?"

"I told the guys because I'm dating them and I don't want to keep secrets from them," I said evenly. "And I needed Fiona's help to get a DNA sample from Gavin Clarke."

"A DNA…" Josiah echoed. "You're out of your mind."

"What if I am?" I spread my hands to either side. "If it shows I'm not related to him, we'll get on with our lives." I dropped my hands to my thighs.

"Doubtful." He crossed his ankles and supported his chin with his fingers forming a V on either side. "You seem like the sort of person who'd keep digging, even when there was nothing left to dig up."

"Are you calling me stubborn?" I said, crossing my arms over my breasts.

"I am absolutely calling you stubborn," he said. "You wouldn't be here otherwise. Tell me something, what are you going to do if that DNA test comes up negative?"

I lowered my arms and exhaled. "I don't know," I admitted. "I don't know what I'm going to do if it comes back positive, either."

"My guess is it starts with the words 'I told you so.'" He crossed his own arms, mimicking my pose. "Right before you tip Gavin's world upside down. Do you think he deserves that?"

"I think he deserves the truth," I said without reservation. "Don't you?"

The side of Josiah's mouth twitched. "I tried to give him the truth. They wouldn't let me near him. They told me he was too fragile to hear anything I had to say."

My heart stuttered. "You didn't get a chance to tell him what you saw?"

"I just said that, didn't I? Doesn't matter; the police would have told him. If he wanted to hear it from me, he could have." He seemed more resigned than resentful.

"Were you close?" I asked. "I know you used to watch her when he was working."

For a moment, I thought he wasn't going to answer. Finally, he said, "He was like an uncle to me. My parents and Coral's used to take turns cooking on Sunday nights. We'd all get together and eat and whatever. Until that day."

"You haven't spoken to him since then. At all?" That seemed harsh. Like they had the perfect little life up here before it was all ripped away.

"What have I said about not feeling sorry for me?" He narrowed his eyes at me. "It was what it was. I let him down. No reason he shouldn't hate me."

"As much as you hate yourself?" I asked. "Although, I still don't think you have anything to hate yourself for."

He rolled his eyes. "So you've told me."

"Connor, Riley and Fiona, they don't think you should hate yourself either," I said. "And before you say it, they don't hate you. The animosity towards you, they were taught by their parents. All of them are old enough to make up their own minds now and they think differently. They supported me in doing the DNA." I didn't add that they would also support me if I *did* him. That was a whole different conversation.

"Big fucking deal." Josiah shrugged. "In case you hadn't noticed, I don't give a shit what they think."

It was my turn to roll my eyes. "In case you hadn't noticed, I don't believe that. Everyone needs human connection, even if they like to think they don't."

"That's very woo-woo of you." He didn't look like he was buying a word of it.

"It's not woo-woo, it's science," I said. "I know it's been a long time since you were at school, but you must remember science." I smiled teasingly. He was only about ten years older than me, but I couldn't resist the jab.

"I was never very good at school. I preferred working with my hands." He raised one of them above his folded arms, showing off calloused, tanned skin. The kind of fingers that could stroke a girl to orgasm without breaking a sweat.

I swallowed. "I'm sure you are. How are you at making coffee? I know you're not used to guests, but it's the polite thing to do."

"I figured you weren't sticking around for long," he said unapologetically.

"I thought I would. It's pretty up here." I turned to let my gaze linger on the creek, and the trees beyond.

"If I make you a coffee, will you go away?" He seemed resigned.

"If you make me a coffee, I'll consider it," I said. That was all I was willing to concede right now. In spite of him being grumpy as fuck, I liked his company. He was both attractive and fascinating. And deep down, vulnerable and hurting. If I couldn't take away the pain, maybe I could ease it somewhat.

He muttered something about me being annoying, but he pulled the door shut behind him and gestured toward his cottage.

"Let's get this over with."

I flashed him a smile over my shoulder as I walked towards his front door. He reached past me to open it and followed me in.

"This is cosy." I stepped carefully across worn hardwood floors and into the living area. Everything was stone and wood, like the cabin in the mountains it actually was. While the Clarke house looked like a little piece of suburban living, this looks like it grew here.

"It's all right." He turned on a coffee machine that sat on the butcher block countertop and pulled out a couple of clay mugs. He sat them both under the spouts, and waited for them to fill.

I wandered around slowly, taking in the pictures on the walls and the shelves full of books.

"I thought this would be familiar, but it's… Not."

"My mother had the place decorated about ten years ago," he said. "*If* you were here before, it looks different."

I nodded slowly and stopped in front of a picture of young Josiah. He couldn't have been more than about ten, but even then he wasn't smiling. He was staring right at the camera like he wished the photographer would hurry up and take the photo. He wore worn jeans and a shirt that looked as though he'd rolled around in the dirt before the photo was taken. Behind him, was an expanse of green land and a high fence.

"Where was this taken?" I asked.

"Double Maple Ranch," he said, glancing over. "My dad used to ride bulls back in the day. He thought I might like to try."

That explained the dirt.

"Were you any good?" I turned around to face him.

"I was okay." He shrugged one shoulder. "According to him, I had the makings of a champion." He seemed indifferent to that.

"You didn't agree?" I asked.

"I'm good at pissing people off. I didn't see the point of pissing off animals too. I preferred riding horses to falling off cattle. I used to think..."

"What did you use to think?" I pressed.

He shook his head. I thought he wasn't going to answer. Finally he said, "I thought it'd be fun to bring some horses up here. Take folks on trail rides through the forest. It was a dumb idea."

"I think it's a great idea," I said. "I'm surprised someone isn't doing that already. I'd be the first to sign up." I might need a bit of help getting up, especially on a bad day, but I could sit on the back of a horse while it walked through the forest. Right? As long as the horse was very slow and very tame. I liked some of the wilder activities I'd done with the guys, but a horse had a mind of its own. They might decide to buck me off if it felt like it. Since I hadn't been on the back of one for years, starting slowly and carefully seemed like the better option.

"Your boyfriends might organise it for you." He turned away to add sweetener to the coffees and stir them quickly. His back was stiff again, defensive. Like he'd spilled his deepest darkest secret to me and then immediately regretted doing it. As if every time he opened a window a crack, he had to close a door with a hard slam and lock it tight.

Except, every time he opened up to me, I felt like I was teasing at his walls, pulling them down bit by bit.

"I think they have enough on their plates." I walked over to take my coffee from his hand and nodded my thanks. "But you never know, that might be something they plan to do someday. Maybe you and I could go for a ride sometime." I watched him over the rim of my cup, seeing him processing my innuendo.

He snorted, sending steam sideways. "Sweet cheeks, you wouldn't be able to handle me."

"You have no idea what I can handle," I said.

Would he believe me if I told him I fucked three guys last night? I wasn't sure if I believed it myself. I hadn't mentioned Brooks to him yet. I would, but so far I hadn't managed to work him into the conversation. How did I approach that anyway? 'By the way, I'm also fucking my stepbrother. You're okay with that, right? And by the way, they want you to join.' Yeah, that was definitely something that had to wait for the right moment.

"You might be right there." He stepped past me and peered out the window. "We might even find out."

"What do you—" I followed his gaze. The snow was falling heavier now. Thicker. Settling on the ground where it lay.

"You wanted that coffee," Josiah pointed out.

Yes I did, but I didn't plan on getting stuck up here.

15

LEAH

"It's really coming down out there." Josiah and I sat on separate armchairs, watching the snow continue to fall through a wide window.

"Next time you pay someone an unwanted visit, check the forecast first." He uncrossed his legs and crossed them the other way.

"It's not supposed to fall this heavily for weeks," I protested. It hadn't crossed my mind to check again.

"Are you sure?" He looked over at me. "You might have looked at the forecast and come here anyway."

"You think I wanted to get stuck here with you on purpose?" I asked. "Wow, you have an ego after all."

"I never said I didn't." He looked back out at the snow. "It'll settle down in an hour or two."

"Then what?" I asked. I could think of worse ways to spend my afternoon than sitting in front of a warm fire, watching the snow fall, a metre or two from an attractive man.

"Then we wait for it to thaw," he said with a smirk.

I raised my eyebrows at him.

He shrugged. "I thought the plan was for you to stay here until spring."

"As long as you have Wi-Fi." I matched his tone.

"Depends on the weather," he said. "Sometimes we do. Sometimes we don't. If I don't, then the lodge will."

"The lodge, right."

"What will your boyfriends think if you spend the winter with me?" He cocked an eyebrow at me.

"They'd probably assume we spent most of it in bed," I said lightly. "What else is there to do up here?"

"Not much else." He looked away again. "Keep the fire going. Cook food once in a while."

"Fire, food and fucking." I could definitely think of worse.

"Then at the first hint of spring, I'll have two meatheads at my door, ready to punch the shit out of me." He grunted at that.

"It might be worth it," I said, half joking. "But there'd be three of them."

He looked over at me again, his brows knitted. "Three?"

"Yeah. I have a thing going with another guy as well."

"Do the first two know about him?" Josiah seemed amused rather than scandalised. Or even surprised.

"Yes, they do," I said. "They all know about each other."

He took a few moments to process that. "You're with all three of them. And you fuck all of them? And they're all okay with this?"

"More than okay," I said. "In fact, they encouraged it. Connor and Riley brought Brooks over with them."

"Brooks? He's new in town?"

"Yes, he's working at the Frosty Brew," I said slowly. "And he's my…stepbrother."

"Okay," Josiah said, equally slowly. "Do they know you're here?"

"I sent them a text when it started snowing," I said. "So, yes. They know I'm here."

He glanced at the door as though they were right

outside at this moment, about to break it down to get to me.

"You said they believed me about what happened to Coral." He turned to me again. "Are they also planning to encourage you to fuck me?"

"Not planning on it," I said. "They've already given me their blessing."

His Adam's apple bobbed. "Connor Ferguson and Riley Crane said they were okay if I fuck you?"

"Yes," I said simply. "They want me to get everything I want. They want me to be happy and satisfied."

Josiah scrubbed a hand over his face. "Are they out of their fucking minds? They've hated me most of their lives, why would they want me anywhere near you?"

"Like I said, they only felt what their parents told them to feel." If Jacob Ferguson and Henry Crane were in front of me right now, I'd give them a piece of my mind. "Now they know better."

"They don't even know me." He dropped his hand to the arm of his chair, gripped it like he might fall off.

"I know you," I said. "They trust my judgement." They'd get to know each other. Connor and Josiah were a lot alike. Both grumpy, but pretending to be bigger assholes than they really were. Brooks too, although the chip on his shoulder was different. As for Riley, he was the glue that held the rest of us together. Maybe nail or screw would be a better metaphor. Something more unyielding than glue.

"You don't know me either," Josiah argued. "I don't know you."

"I know you're a good person, deep down," I said. Just because he didn't see it, didn't mean it wasn't true. The same could be said for the other three as well. Possibly even myself.

He snorted in response to that.

"You are," I insisted. "You were dealt a shitty hand, there's no denying that. Maybe I was too. But we can't let the past define everything we do. At some point, we have to let it go and live in the present. We might even be daring and…" I paused for dramatic effect. "Think about the future."

"You're delusional," he told me. "The past is everything. It makes us who we are. The choices we make, the things we say and do. I could have told them I saw her fall in the creek and everything would have been different. I could have gone along with what they said. Do you have any idea how much easier that would have made…everything? I could have told them I looked away for a second and she ran off. I could have told them anything. Made up some bullshit that made me look better. Maybe I should have."

He rubbed his temples with his long fingers. His nails were ragged, but clean. Like he worked with his hands, but took care to wash away the signs of it.

"But you didn't, because that's not who you are," I said. I pushed myself to my feet and moved to kneel on the rug in front of his chair. It was so thick, my knees sank into it. I took a moment to be grateful it wasn't hardwood, but I would have done the same if it was. I needed him to see me and to understand. To really listen. "You were honest."

"I was an idiot," he snapped. "What fucking use was the truth? Who did it help? Not me. Not her. Not you, whether you're her or not."

I placed my hands on his knees. "What use would lying have been? You would have had to live with that lie all these years. Don't tell me that wouldn't have eaten you up?"

"I told you not to feel sorry for me," he growled softly. "I fucked up. End of story."

"It's not the end—" I started.

His arm snapped out and he grabbed a handful of my hair. "It's the fucking end. If you don't stop I'm going to…"

"What are you going to do?" I whispered. My pulse was racing, clit fluttering. My nipples were already hard. The anticipation made me wet as hell.

His eyes were dark as they looked back at me. Darker still when his hand tightened around my hair. With the other, he pushed down the front of his track pants and boxer briefs, letting his erection spring free.

My eyes widened. The underside of his cock was decorated with four metal bars, each a few millimetres apart. Pre-cum already leaked from his tip.

He pushed my face forward, until my lips were pressed against his crown.

"You want to fuck me?" His voice was ragged. "Open your fucking mouth and suck my cock."

I flicked my tongue out, licking the tip, tasting the slick salt on his heated skin.

He groaned. "Leah…" He pushed my face forward more, until I opened my mouth. Then he was sliding his cock between my lips, just the tip at first, then gradually more.

His piercings were smooth against my lips. I stroked my tongue over them instinctively.

"You want to know why I got those?" he asked, each word more strained than the one before. "Because they hurt like a bitch. I wanted them to. I wanted to hurt. I deserved to hurt."

I looked up at him sharply, but his eyes were closed as he started to roll his hips, thrusting, fucking my mouth slowly. I wrapped my fingers around the base of his cock, stroking his balls and pumping him in rhythm with his strokes. Wanting to bring him to orgasm. Wanting to see him shatter. To taste him on my tongue.

"Fucking hell," he whispered. "Your fucking mouth..." He thrust faster a couple of times before coming, squirting his release into the back of my throat.

I gagged and then managed to swallow, continuing to stroke him until he finally let out a long breath and slid his cock free.

At the same time, he let go of my hair and sat back.

"Shit, Leah... I shouldn't have... Fuck." He ran a hand over the back of his head. "I'm sorry, I—" He screwed his eyes shut.

"Yes, you should." I teased around the tip of his cock with my tongue and smiled. "I wanted you to. If I didn't, I would have told you."

He regarded me for a moment. "Get back in your chair and let me fuck you with my mouth." He knew I was right. If I wanted to say no, I would, but I liked his assertiveness. If he told me to lie out in the snow with my legs spread so he could fuck me out there, I would have. My blood was so hot I might melt it right down to the ground.

Without hesitation, I pushed myself to my feet and retook my seat. He knelt in front of me, grabbed my leggings and panties and yanked them down my legs and off over my shoes. I barely had time to blink before he dipped his head between my thighs and started to devour me.

I moaned. "Josiah… Yes, just there." I felt like he was going to eat me alive. And I was here for it. I was here for it when he pulled down the front of my shirt and bra and palmed my breast. Pinching my nipple when it became harder still.

He slid a calloused finger into me, then another, hooking them around to stroke me from the inside while relentlessly sucking my clit.

I bucked against his mouth as he pushed me closer and closer to coming. The stubble on his chin scratching the inside of my thighs, the perfect amount of tension. The perfect amount of… everything.

I arched my back as I shattered against his tongue, crying out his name over and over, wanting to make it last. Blood raced through my veins and pounded in my ears. For the longest time, everything disappeared except bliss that started in my toes and travelled all the way up to my head. Consuming everything.

He didn't stop when I started to come down, instead pushing me, stroking me, licking me until the pressure started to build again.

"Josiah…" I whispered. "I don't know if I can." Then I was back on the edge of the precipice, my toes curled, ready to pitch over again.

I gripped the arms of the chair, holding on as I broke into a million pieces, screaming out his name so loud I wouldn't have been surprised if they heard it right at the bottom of the mountain. Loud enough to make the earth move and my throat hurt. I cried out and cried out until finally I flopped back, boneless and panting.

"That was…incredible," I said when I finally managed to speak again.

"It was what you deserve," he said. He kissed the insides of my thighs as though worshipping them, then rested the side of his face on my leg.

"I'm not good enough for you," he said softly.

"Yes, you are," I told him. "I might not be good enough for you."

Before he could respond, the sound of engines approaching broke through the otherwise silent room.

16

—————

LEAH

Josiah's eyes swivelled to the door. "Fuck." He hurried to put my panties and leggings back in place, then fixed his own clothes.

"Who is it?" I twisted my upper body around to look, before pushing myself to my feet.

He glanced through a window that looked out to the front of the house. "Take a wild guess."

"Oh." It didn't take a genius to figure it out.

Josiah looked back over his shoulder. "Yeah, oh."

I stood beside him as Connor's truck pull in beside my car. Of course his was better equipped for the snow than mine. I should have realised that. Their job included making their way around the mountain in conditions like this. If it wasn't his truck, it would have been a snowmobile.

"Looks like they've come to rescue you." Josiah sounded bitter, like he was contemplating keeping the door locked against them.

"I could have told them I don't need rescuing," I said, placing a hand on his shoulder. "Turns out, you're not the big bad wolf after all."

He grunt-laughed. "If you believe that, I haven't worked hard enough. I should have bitten you harder."

"You didn't bite me," I pointed out.

"Yet." He leaned over and nipped my earlobe.

"I stand corrected, you are the big bad wolf," I teased. I turned back to the window and watched Connor, Riley and Brooks climb out of the truck. Connor looked irritated to be here. Brooks looked irritated at the presence of snow. And Riley, he was grinning like it was already Christmas morning.

"Does that make them the three little pigs?" Josiah asked.

"I dare you to call them that," I said with a straight face.

He smirked.

"Or you could all be nice to each other," I said. "Are you going to open the door?"

He looked like he might refuse, but he moved

over to unlock it. He waited for a beat or two, swinging it inwards as Connor was about to knock.

Connor stopped with his fist in the air, but managed not to pitch forward into the cottage. Eyes flashing with further irritation, he lowered his hand.

"Leah, what are you doing here?" He eyed me and Josiah, as if he could tell what we'd just been doing.

"Catching him up on things," I said lightly. Which was exactly the purpose for my visit. I wasn't going to apologise for it.

"Can we come in? It's cold out here." Brooks rubbed his hands together.

Josiah stepped back to let them in, muttering something that sounded like, "Little pig, little pig."

Holding back a laugh, I gave each of them a hug as they stepped inside.

"This is cosy." Riley took a good look around.

"It's all right." Josiah shrugged. He wandered over to the kitchen to put on more coffee.

I quickly made the introductions before they all got comfortable. Brooks sat right in front of the fire, so close he was almost sitting in it.

"Who is this guy?" my stepbrother asked.

I exchanged glances with Connor and Riley before deciding now was as good a time as any to explain everything to Brooks. Using as few words as possible, I told him everything I knew. Right down to the DNA test I sent off.

"What the fuck?" Brooks squinted at me. "You think you're some kid that went missing?"

"I don't know," I said. "That's what I'm trying to find out." I was sixteen when he and I met, so all of this happened long before we knew each other. Unless my mother confided in him, then he knew as much as I did.

"This is wild." He ran a hand through his blonde curls. "You're not actually related to any of these guys, are you?"

That was met with a stunned silence before all three of them shook their heads.

"Unlikely," Connor said.

"Not a chance." Josiah handed cups of coffee around. "My parents never would have cheated on each other."

"Mine probably wouldn't either, but I don't give a shit," Riley said. "Even if Leah is my half-sister, it doesn't change anything." He shrugged when we all turned to look at him. "I feel how I feel, okay?"

"That's fucked up, bro," Connor said.

"I don't care." Riley crossed his legs at his knees, not backing down an inch. "Like I said, it's not likely, so this conversation is unnecessary."

I had a feeling he might feel differently if he actually was my half brother, but that was a whole other can of worms. One we didn't need to open right now.

"So, you believe her." Josiah lowered himself back into the chair where he was sitting when I had my mouth around his cock.

"Yes, we do," Connor said. "Is there any reason why we shouldn't?"

"None at all," Josiah said coldly. "You didn't believe me. Seems like a sudden change of heart."

"We were dicks," Riley admitted.

"Yes, you were," Josiah said flatly. "Why shouldn't I throw you back out into the snow?" The question was rhetorical and he got no answer other than a snort or two.

"Seems your nickname was appropriate," Connor said calmly. "You really did dash after a car to stop them from taking Coral."

"Don't fucking start with that nickname," Josiah growled.

"Who's starting anything?" Connor shrugged one shoulder as if he wasn't shit disturbing the whole time.

"That would be you," I told him. "I know being

nice to each other is new, but maybe you could try it. You might even like it."

All three men gave each other doubtful looks.

Brooks caught my eye and made a face like he wondered what the hell I was doing with them.

I rubbed the heel of my hand over my forehead. No one ever said this was going to be easy.

"Do you want them to leave?" Josiah asked. "Because I have no trouble kicking their asses back out the door."

"Only if you want your ass kicked." Connor looked about ready to start swinging punches.

"No one is kicking anyone's ass," I said. "Kissing is optional."

Josiah and Connor grunted in unison.

"Is it me, or are they both hot?" Riley whispered loudly.

I smiled. "They both are. You all are. I care about all of you. I'd like to try to make this work between us, but if you can't get along…"

"Then you can come back to Vancouver with me," Brooks finished for me.

"Not without me," Riley said quickly. "Except, I'm not leaving. So you both have to stay."

"I'm not going anywhere either." Connor gave Josiah the side eye.

Josiah gave it right back, before letting out a long, slow breath. "Look, I can try to put the past behind us, but since you were the asshole all this time, you need to make a fucking effort."

Connor was on his feet, hands curled into fists. "I didn't—"

Josiah rose as well, standing chest to chest with the other man. "You fucking did. I know you were only listening to what you were told. That's the reason you're standing here right now. You didn't know any fucking better. Now you do."

Connor looked like he wanted to argue, but he hardened his jaw and lowered his hands. "I'm making an effort." He sat back down.

Josiah regarded him for a few moments before he too sat back down.

"That was hot," Riley said.

Brooks looked conflicted. "I've heard about mountain men…"

"We're even better than anything you've heard," Riley said.

"I think I can see that," Brooks said softly. He still looked confused.

For a moment, I wondered why, then it dawned on me. He'd just figured something about himself that he hadn't known before. He wasn't just attracted to women. I had to admit, there was something about these men that would make it difficult to ignore those urges. I certainly couldn't.

"I know this isn't going to be easy," I said slowly. "There's a lot of water… Maybe that isn't such a good expression to use in this situation." I winced. "A lot of history between Connor, Riley and Josiah. And history between Brooks and me. If this is going to work, then we need to learn to communicate with each other."

"I'm down," Riley said. "I admit this is weird. It wasn't that long ago that the idea of you even talking to Josiah made me want to punch him in the face. But shit changes and I'll roll with it."

"Whatever," Connor muttered. "I'm not giving Leah up."

"Neither am I," Brooks said quickly.

Josiah scrubbed his face with his hand. "Do I have a choice?"

"There's always a choice," I told him. "I know you feel the connection between us. I do too. I'd like to see where it can go. If you don't want to, then…"

He looked thoughtful for a solid minute before saying, "I do want to. As long as those two keep their heads out of their asses." He nodded toward Connor in particular.

"Back at you," Connor told him. "You weren't innocent in all of this. Yeah, we gave you shit, but you gave it back."

"Wouldn't you do the fucking same?" Josiah demanded. "If everyone told you to stay the hell away from Aurora Hollow, how the hell would you act? You'd come out swinging."

"Josiah is right," Riley said softly, as though worried he was going to spark an inferno in the form of Connor's temper. "We were shitheads. Classic case of monkey see, monkey do. Worse, we knew the way our fathers talked to, and *about* him was wrong, and we copied it anyway."

"Allegedly," Connor said. "We still don't have proof he's telling the truth."

Josiah glared at him. "If you're going to be a prick—"

"Okay," I snapped. "Can we all calm down?"

"It's not too late to go back to Vancouver," Brooks said.

All three of the other guys turned to him, and in unison said, "No."

"At least they agree on something," I said with a sigh.

"We should get back to town before the roads

become slipperier and we need a snowplough to get out of here," Connor said.

Josiah gave him a look to suggest he could have stayed in town if he'd wanted to. "The snow has stopped falling. You'll be fine."

I glanced at the window to see he was right. How long had it been? I hadn't noticed it stop.

"I was hoping for a blizzard," Riley said with a sigh. "Half of that will be melted by morning."

"Good," Brooks said, rubbing his hands together as if they were still cold. They looked red from the fire.

"Don't worry, it'll be snowing its ass off properly in no time," Riley told him, knowing he'd get a rise out of Brooks.

He was right. Brooks looked at him like he was out of his mind.

"You'll be too busy at the pub to give a shit," Connor said. For the first time since they arrived, he actually seemed pleased about something. Of course he did, he no longer had to worry about his father insisting he take over from him. As long as Brooks was around, he was off that hook.

"I can't wait," Brooks said. He spoke with a hint of sarcasm, but he looked genuinely excited to take up the challenge. I couldn't remember having seen that expression on his face. Like for once in his life he wasn't being forced to do something he hated.

I was happy for him. For Connor too. And Riley, because I knew he wanted to grow their business as much as Connor did.

And Josiah? Things were going to take longer for him. Once we had all the answers we needed, the whole town would know the truth. I didn't expect them to welcome him back with open arms straight away. For that to happen, they'd have to admit they were wrong.

That might be the biggest hurdle of all.

17

LEAH

"LET ME GET THIS STRAIGHT," Whitney said slowly, cutting the occasional glance toward the bar. "He's your stepbrother and he's working for Connor and his dad."

"That's right," I said. "Connor thought he could take over as manager so Brooks is here, learning how to pull beer." He'd been busy all night, running back and forth, serving customers. The Frosty Brew was packed full of locals and visitors. There was barely enough room to turn around, but Brooks looked like he was loving every minute of it.

"And Brooks is one of your boyfriends now too?" Holly asked.

"We haven't talked about it, but it seems so," I said. "We're going to see how things go."

"And Josiah as well." Fiona looked impressed. "Woman, you are *goals*." She raised her glass to me.

"You can say that again," Holly agreed. "Where do you sign up for this program?"

We all laughed.

"I guess I got lucky," I said. "Four boyfriends and three best friends. What more could a girl want?"

Fiona opened her mouth, glanced at the other two women and closed it again.

I could guess what she was thinking. A girl could want results for the DNA test. I took in a long breath and blurted out as much about Coral Clarke as I could before I ran out of air and had to inhale.

Whitney and Holly both stared at me.

"Are you kidding me?" Whitney asked. "Of all the things I thought you might say, that wasn't even on the list."

"Me either," Holly said. She raised a hand. "You're going to have to give me a minute or two here."

"I'll take three or four," Whitney said. "Wow." She blinked a couple of times and shook her head. "You knew about this?" She said to Fiona. "You don't look surprised."

"I only found out the other day," Fiona said. "For the record, I'm still trying to process it. But I'm glad you both know now. No offence, Leah, but I hated keeping secrets from them."

"So did I." I drank a gulp of wine to steady my nerves. They still might tell me I was out of my mind. "It's a difficult conversation to bring up, you know?"

Whitney leaned over to put a hand on my forearm. "Hey, it's okay. We get it. We're not judging you for holding out on us. Right Holly?"

"Yeah. I mean, I guess so," Holly said slowly. "It still might not be true, though. You don't know for sure?"

"No," I admitted. "I don't. I felt like you should know in case it is. So I'm not dropping a bombshell on you later."

"I was just recovering from the four boyfriends part," Holly said. "I can't decide if I'm too drunk or too sober for this conversation." She ended the last word on a laugh.

"Me too." I took another gulp of wine. "I'm still trying to make sense of it all myself." If that was even possible. Some day I might look back and this would be nothing, but right now it was…everything.

"You remember some things about Aurora Hollow," Whitney said slowly. "Do you remember any of us?" She gestured around the table.

"I don't know," I said. "My earliest memory is my mother yelling at me for dropping a cupcake on the carpet." I frowned. "I couldn't figure out why she was so angry. That was in Vancouver."

"You would have been at school here for a little while," Whitney said. "Maybe in the classroom where you helped me out that day, with the art class. You don't remember that place?"

I frowned deeper and thought back, but eventually shook my head. "No, I don't. It seemed familiar, but it looked like every other classroom I've been in."

"Right," Whitney said thoughtfully. "But you might have been there long enough to be in a class photo."

I sat up higher and stared at her. "I might have." Why hadn't I thought of that? "Do you know where I could find one?"

"My mother would have some, but they're probably right in the back of the attic," Fiona said regretfully.

"We don't have any, we had a house fire," Holly said softly.

I shot her a sympathetic look and a faint smile which she responded to with a shrug.

"It was a long time ago."

"The school would have them," Whitney said.

"Come on, let's go and look." She hopped down from her stool.

I stared at her. "Now?"

"You really want to wait until Monday?" She cocked her head at me. "I have keys. It's only a five minute walk now the snow has all melted again."

"I..." I was eager, but scared at the same time. Scared of what I might see in those photos, or what I might *not* see. Although, this could put the whole matter to rest tonight. I might not need the results of the DNA test. An hour from now, I could know more about my past. Another piece of the puzzle in place.

"Let's do it," I said finally. I finished the last of my wine and followed her toward the door, waving at Connor and Riley who sat at a table with some of their friends, to let them know I was leaving.

Connor nodded and let his gaze linger on my mouth before returning to his conversation.

"I feel like a secret agent," Fiona said from behind me. "Sneaking out on a secret mission."

Holly, who was right behind her, giggled. "Super secret, sneaking out in front of all these people."

Fiona snorted. "Hey, don't ruin the moment." She was smiling at the same time. She hurried to catch up, so all four of us were walking together, in a line.

"We definitely aren't subtle," Whitney said. "All of us are too cute to be subtle."

"Amen to that," Fiona said.

"Whitney over there speaking truths," Holly agreed.

"Whitney always speaks truths," Whitney said. "Whitney is very wise."

"Whitney is talking about herself in third person," Fiona pointed out. "Some people would say that's weird."

"Some people can fuck off," Whitney laughed. "We all know how cool I am."

"Yeah, we do." Holly tripped over a crack in the sidewalk and Fiona had to grab her to stop her from falling. "I think I might be on the 'too drunk' side of things after all." She giggled.

I grinned. She'd had more to drink than I did, which was probably a good thing given we were about to enter a school.

"We're not breaking and entering, are we?" I asked.

"Nah." Whitney reached into her bag and pulled out a set of keys. Before she put one in the lock, she turned off the alarm system with a code, tapped into the screen beside the door. "See, all good, eh." She pushed the door open and stepped inside, leaving us to follow.

The whole place was quiet and dark, our footsteps echoing on the floor as we walked toward the front office.

Whitney pulled out another key and unlocked the door before flicking on the light.

"They keep them organised by years," she said. "You'd be two years below me." She stepped over to a wall of shelves, each with its own box labelled with past years. There must have been thirty years of boxes here, with room for another decade.

She pulled out one and carried it over to a table. Sliding off the lid, she set it aside and started to rummage through the contents.

"They keep all sorts of random things in here." She pulled out a yellowed flyer, announcing a school dance for the older kids in the school.

"I'm starting to feel old." Fiona squinted at the flyer before putting it back down on the table.

"Here we go, class photos. Grade five. Grade four…" Whitney put them to one side before saying, "Okay, here we go." She held up an envelope, opened one end and tipped it up, letting the photos slide out.

"It's me." Fiona caught up one and held it for us to

see. She had pigtail sticking up to either side of her head and a huge grin on her face.

"Awww, so cute," Holly said. "Hey, there's a class photo." She eased it out from under the others and we all gathered around to look.

"That's me." Fiona pointed. "And that's Holly. There's Connor, hiding behind everyone else like he doesn't want to be seen."

He was adorable, with short hair and a scowl on his face. Right beside him, I recognised Riley. He was looking at something in front of him, not at the camera.

"That's Coral," Fiona said softly. She pointed at a little girl sitting right at the front, wearing a purple T-shirt with a unicorn on it. Her hair was up in a braid and she was smiling, sitting beside another girl.

"Holy shit," Whitney whispered. She looked from the photo to me and back again. "That's definitely you. Same face shape. Same hair colour. Same eye colour."

I had to agree. If I wasn't Coral Clarke, I was the spitting image of her. But there was more to it than that.

"I have photos of me at around that age and I

look the same," I also whispered. "Except in those photos, I'm not smiling." This little girl looked happy. Like she had no idea what was about to happen to her.

"I think that settles it," Whitney said. She took out her phone and took a photo of the class photograph before sliding it back in the envelope and putting it back in the box.

"What do we do now?" Holly asked. "Do we tell everyone?"

"I think I'd like to wait for the DNA test to come back first," I said. "If we show people that, they might think we're reaching. Just because she looks like me doesn't mean she *is* me."

"I think that's a good idea," Fiona said. "Once you have proof, we can explain things to everyone. Don't worry, we've got you." She wrapped her arms around me and squeezed. "Whatever happens, we'll be here for you."

I squeezed her back. "Thank you. I don't know what I'd do without you three." Or my four boyfriends.

"Saturday nights would be a lot less interesting." Whitney slid the box back into place and turned off the light. "We should get out of here before someone comes."

"I thought you said we weren't breaking and entering," Fiona said, following the rest of us out of the office.

"We're not. That doesn't mean we should be here," Whitney said. "They don't usually like teachers sneaking around the place in the middle of the night on a Saturday." She locked the door behind us and re-engaged the security system.

"Tell them you were preparing for class on Monday," Holly said, half joking. "They'll think you're conscientious."

Whitney barked a ha. "They know me better than that. I love my job, but I wouldn't be here on a Saturday for no reason. Especially Saturday night. Especially when Morgan Hardwick is in town. Speaking of him, we should get back to the pub. He usually plays a set when he's around."

"The country singer?" I asked. He was ridiculously famous. According to the gossip pages on the Internet, he had a house around here somewhere, but I didn't realise it was in this town. Or that he performed at the pub.

"Hell yeah I do." Whitney hooked an arm through mine and another through Fiona's. Walking like that, we made our way back to the Frosty Brew, ready to have some fun, even though my head was still spinning from looking at that photograph.

There didn't seem to be much doubt now. I really was Coral Clarke.

Wasn't I?

18

LEAH

"Is that you all you have?" I looked down at the suitcase Brooks was rolling behind him.

"That's all I brought to town with me." He shrugged and let the wheels rattle over the hardwood floor. "I might go home and get more stuff when I get a chance." He didn't look like he was in a hurry to get back there.

"Yeah, me too," I said quietly. "Unless Mom threw it all out already."

"Neither of us is her biggest fan, but I don't see Felicity doing that," he said. "It would require effort on her part."

"She'd also have to notice I wasn't there," I said on a sigh. "You can put your things in the spare room. There's a bed in there already for you."

"Fuck that." He wheeled his suitcase into my room and hefted it onto the bed before opening it and starting to pull out his clothes. "I'll sleep in here with you."

"He's a presumptuous prick," Connor said from where he stood in the kitchen, cooking burgers with Riley.

Brooks rolled his eyes, but didn't stop unpacking.

"I think Brooks would like to say it takes one to know one," I teased, without taking my eyes off my stepbrother.

That was met with the sound of Riley's laughter.

"She's got you there."

"Fuck off," Connor said, maybe to him and maybe to all of us.

"When's Josiah coming?" Brooks asked, without glancing my way.

"He should be here soon." Unless he decided not to come. He'd spent so long avoiding coming into town unless he had to, an invitation to eat dinner here might be too much, too fast. If that was the case, I'd be disappointed, but I'd understand.

I didn't think it would stop the other three from heading up to his place to drag him down here. Just for my sake, that was. Because they knew I wanted all of them here.

"You like him, don't you?" I asked, giving Brooks a cagey look.

He went on unpacking without missing a beat. "He's okay."

"Mmm-hmm." I leaned against the door frame and watched him. "It's okay to like someone, you know? You can even like me if you want to."

He grunted softly. "Why would I do that? You're a pain in my ass. You have been since my dad married your mother."

"The feeling is mutual," I said. "Bad enough that she got married without bringing an asshole along."

"So fucking inconsiderate." He tossed a couple of pairs of shoes on the bottom of the wardrobe and closed it. "You know why my father chose your mother though, right?" He swung his suitcase up to the top of the wardrobe and turned to face me.

"Because she's got an amazing daughter?" I asked, jokingly.

He stalked towards me. "Because he wanted me to have you." He placed his hands on my hips and pulled me flush against him. "You were my wedding present from him, you just didn't know it until now."

"Is that right?" I looked up into his eyes. They were dark and full of fire, heavily laced with arrogance.

"Yes," he said simply.

"So, if I didn't exist, he wouldn't have married her?" I cocked my head at him.

He shrugged. "Maybe he cares about your mother, but your pussy was always mine." He slammed his lips down onto mine, kissing me like he could devour me on the spot. His fingers dug into my hips.

I hooked my arms around his neck and kissed him back, his growing erection pressing into my stomach.

"Brooks—" I was interrupted by a firm knock at the door.

"Ignore it." He pulled me closer.

"That'll be Josiah," I argued. "We can finish this later. Maybe with him too."

Groaning softly, Brooks stepped back and adjusted his pants. "Yeah, okay. I guess I can wait. This time."

"So magnanimous," I teased. I stepped out of the room and hurried to the front door, opening up to see Josiah standing outside. He was facing towards the street, his back rod-straight, like he wanted to be anywhere but here.

"Hey," I said softly. "I'm glad you came."

He turned around like a startled bear, drinking

me in with his eyes. "Hey. I almost didn't. I figured…" He shrugged one shoulder.

"I'm glad you did." I grabbed his hand and pulled him inside. His leather and pine scent, was heady, like he came from the mountain itself.

"The whole gang is here," Riley said, grabbing out plates for everyone.

"Very fucking cosy." Connor flipped a burger and poked it with the spatula. "Won't be long."

"Beer?" Riley opened the fridge and pulled out five before opening them and handing them around.

I nodded my thanks and took one from him. Looking around at the four of them, they all wore dark jeans. Riley with a dark blue hoodie. Josiah was in a leather jacket that looked like it had seen better years. Connor and Brooks both wore black T-shirts, which threatened to burst at the seams around their chests and biceps.

Each of them was a perfect example of the expression 'sex on legs.' And all of them were mine.

"Show Josiah the photo," Riley said. When Josiah gave him a funny look, Riley nodded to me. "The rest of us have seen it, but I'm guessing you haven't."

"I haven't had a chance to show him yet." I pulled out my phone and showed him the photo Whitney sent to me. I didn't need to explain it to him. He knew immediately.

He took the phone from me and enlarged it, for a better look at Coral. "Fuck," he whispered. "I should have seen it sooner." He held it up beside me, looking from the screen to my face and back again several times. "You look just like her."

"Look how cute I was back then," Riley said. "Almost as cute as I am now." He grinned and flexed, careful not to spill any beer.

Brooks snorted. "If you say so."

"I say so," Riley agreed.

"I fucking say so too," Connor growled.

Riley grinned. "See? Connor thinks I'm cute."

I patted his cheek. "You're very cute."

"So are you." He swiped his lips over mine, before deepening the kiss and slipping his tongue between my lips.

"We can all agree Leah is cute," Brooks said.

"A minute ago, you called me a pain in your ass." I took back my phone when Josiah handed it to me. I'd noticed him sending the photo to his own phone.

"You can be both," Brooks said. "Aren't women good at multitasking?"

"Yes, we are," I said. "Look, I can flip you off with both hands and hold a beer bottle at the same time."

"Mad skills," Riley laughed.

"I try." I gave him a careful bow from the waist.

"You can say that again." Brooks smirked. "You've always tried my patience."

I snorted loudly. "That's bullshit and you know it. You don't have any patience."

He opened and closed his mouth a couple of times before grunting. "Okay, I'll give you that. But if I had patience, you'd try it."

"We all know he loves her," Riley whispered loudly.

"No shit." Connor started to place the burgers on plates and carried them over to the table. "We all do."

I looked at him in surprise. I hadn't expected him to make that sort of declaration, especially not in front of everyone else.

"Yeah, we do," Josiah said softly. "Even if some of us tried not to."

"I didn't try not to," Riley said. "I love Leah and I love Connor."

"Love you too," Connor muttered.

"I'm falling for all of you," I said after a couple of moments of getting my emotions under control. "You guys are all amazing."

"No, you." Riley put his arms around my shoulder

and guided me over to the table. "You've been standing long enough. Sit."

He was right, I was and I was starting to feel it. Gratefully, I sat and watched all of them take their places around me.

A girl could get used to this.

"Eat." Connor placed a fresh beer in front of me and took his own seat. I almost missed his hint of anxiety as he glanced at my burger. He was worried I might not like it, or his cooking wouldn't be up to my expectations. Judging by the smell, it was going to taste incredible.

I picked up my burger and took a bite, moaning at the taste. "Are you sure you shouldn't be a chef?"

The side of his mouth twitched up in a hint of a smile. "I'm sure, but glad you like it."

"Connor makes the best burgers on the whole continent," Riley said.

"They're all right," Brooks said.

Connor bristled. "All—"

"He's trying to get a rise out of you," I told him. "Ignore him. He's a shit disturber from way back."

Connor muttered something that sounded like 'he's a fucking prick,' but he settled back in his chair and started eating.

Josiah gave me a look like he wasn't sure what he'd signed up for with the other guys.

I reached over to pat his arm. "They'll get used to each other."

"If they don't kill each other first," he said softly. "On the other hand, that leaves more of you for me." He didn't seem to mind that too much. Of course he wouldn't, sharing with three other guys was a big deal. Especially when we'd just started to get to know each other.

I couldn't help thinking about his piercings, wondering how they'd feel inside my pussy. The idea of the additional friction was enough to make me wet as hell. I didn't like the idea he got them to punish himself, but I'd reap the benefits of their presence. And, I hoped, so would he. Piercings were supposed to give additional sensitivity, weren't they? Who knows, he might even inspire the others to get piercings as well. If they wanted to, they had my complete support. I might even get my nipples pierced the next time I was in the city. Why not live a little?

"And me," Riley said, breaking through my thoughts. He'd probably be first in line to have his cock pierced if any of them did. And possibly his nipples as well. I could easily imagine him naked, with glittering metal in various places on his muscular body. Unless of course they were a safety issue during extreme sport.

"No one is killing me," Connor said. "Not even that dickhead."

"What he said." Brooks gave him a dark look. At the same time, he seemed to be enjoying himself. As if he were starting to see the others like brothers, complete with brotherly banter. With the bonus of a hint of desire for them to tear each other's clothes off and fuck until they were both boneless.

"Just think, I could have grown up with these three." I jerked a thumb toward Connor, Riley and Josiah.

"Instead, you got to meet me," Brooks said. "I guess the universe knew something."

"The universe has some questions to answer," I said. "So does my mother." That brought the mood down immediately. If I was Coral Clarke, how had I ended up with Felicity Kent? I hadn't wanted to think about it before now, but at some point I'd have to face facts. Facts I didn't want to dwell on right now. Not if it meant ruining tonight.

"We're here now," Riley said. "That's what matters. Whatever goes down, we've got your back."

"What he said," Brooks said again.

"You belong to us, that's the important thing," Connor said. "Finish your burger so we can have dessert." He pointed a finger at Riley as he opened his mouth. "I mean actual dessert, then we'll fuck her."

"Works for me." Riley grinned. "I can't wait to get all of you naked."

That brought the mood right back up. Because neither could I.

19

JOSIAH

I COULDN'T REMEMBER the last time I was around so many people. Especially when none of those people where telling me to leave.

Underneath my skin itched, waiting for those words. Waiting for someone to realise I was here, where I didn't belong. Both Connor and Riley occasionally gave me glances, reminding me of the amount of times they'd said those words.

Tonight, I got the impression they regretted them, although neither was going out of their way to say sorry. Instead, they were acting like this was the new normal and there was nothing to question about it. The past couldn't be erased, but we could move on.

If they thought I wouldn't bring it up at some

point, they were out of their minds. For now though, I kept my peace and so did they. All that mattered right now was Leah.

"Let's get this cleaned up." Connor stood and started to gather up bowls.

"That was so good." Riley patted his stomach.

I had to admit Connor's homemade apple pie and ice cream was surprisingly delicious. I'd say I had no idea he could cook like that, but what did I really know about him anyway? Not much outside the adventure tours. We never had a conversation that wasn't hostile.

"It was amazing." Leah stood and started to help, before Connor waved her off.

Taking the initiative, I grabbed her wrist and drew her over to the couch. Before any of them could say or do anything, I sat with her on my lap, my arms around her.

She twisted around to look at me and smile, making my heart thud in my chest. "Hey there."

I brushed hair off the side of her face.

"Hey." *Very eloquent*, Josiah. I wasn't a man of many words to start with. Tonight, I'd used up my quota and then some. I wanted to rely on another method of communication instead.

I cupped the back of her head and held her there

while I lowered my mouth to hers. Tasting her sweet, plush lips. I pressed my tongue between them, insisting on access. She opened her mouth, letting me inside, her tongue stroking mine.

I dropped my hand to her back, sliding it up under her shirt. Savouring the smooth expanse of skin before I flicked open the hooks of her bra.

"Leave some for me." Brooks sat beside me and turned her face to him so he could taste her mouth.

While they kissed, I worked her shirt up to her neck. They had to break off so he and I could pull it over her head and out of the way. The straps of her bra slid down her arms, letting her breasts fall free.

"Fuck, she's pretty," Brooks said.

I gave him a sharp look. "She's beautiful."

"You guys aren't bad yourselves," she said with a soft laugh.

"I'm okay," I said with a sideways look down toward the floor.

"You're better than okay, right Brooks?" she insisted.

I raised my gaze to look at both of them, just as Brooks replied with a short nod. I didn't expect him to say anything more, and he didn't, but the look he gave me said more than words would have anyway.

"Thanks," I muttered awkwardly. Now would be a good time to busy myself cupping Leah's breasts and palming her nipples, making them harder for me.

"Josiah," Leah said, soft but insistent again. "Look at me."

"I am looking at you." I rolled her nipples between my thumbs and forefingers.

"Look at my *face*." She tilted her head, so she could look me in the eyes.

I managed to drag my eyes from her breasts, to meet her gaze. "You don't need to—"

"I think I do," she said. "You deserve to be loved as much as the rest of us. Maybe more than some of us." She slid a teasing look toward Brooks.

"Fuck off," he said with a laugh. "I know you love me."

She leaned over and kissed his mouth before turning back to me. "If this is too much, too soon, we understand. It's a big deal to go from being alone, to being part of a group. No one would blame you if you need to step away."

"You're right," I said, my voice low, as if that might keep me from being judged. "It's a lot. I want to be here." Wherever she was, I wanted to be there too. "If you want me to be."

"We want you here," she said firmly. "I want all of you here."

"Even me?" Brooks ran the tip of his finger down the side of her face, over her collarbone and down to her chest, stopping just short of my hand.

"Even you," she whispered, her eyes darkening.

"I think she's overdressed, don't you agree, Josiah?" Brooks asked.

"I definitely agree," I said. "I think we should fix that immediately." Reluctantly, I moved my hands from her breasts, down to her waist, lifting her carefully so Brooks could ease her leggings and panties down over her ass. She had to straighten her legs so he could pull them off her feet and toss them aside.

"Much better." Brooks pulled her feet into his lap and started to run his hands up the inside of her legs.

I let my gaze slide up and down her body, taking in every curve, every freckle. Wanting to commit every centimetre of her to memory. She was so beautiful, she made my cock harder than hell. Pressing into the side of her ass.

"Perfect," I whispered, so soft I could barely hear it myself.

"I bet she's nice and wet already." Brooks teased her thighs apart.

"Show us." Connor and Riley finished placing

bowls in the dishwasher and had come to join us. Connor crouched in front of me and Brooks. "Show us how wet she is."

Brooks carefully bent her knees, opening her legs out to them.

Connor's tongue slid across his lower lip. "So wet."

"Very wet." Brooks' fingers were on her pussy, pressing into her. It drew a moan from her plush lips.

Making me even harder.

"If one of you doesn't—" she started.

"We'll tell you when one of us will fuck you," Connor said.

"Who died and made you boss?" Brooks circled her clit with his thumb.

"I made myself boss," Connor said. He pulled out his phone and started filming the way he was touching her.

"Josiah and I are both older than you," Brooks pointed out.

Without moving his phone too much, Connor shrugged a shoulder. "I don't give a shit. Make her come."

If Brooks looked irritated at being given an order, it didn't stop him from carrying it out.

Rubbing and stroking her, coaxing her toward orgasm while I lavished attention on her breasts, keeping her nipples hard with my fingers.

Her back arched into me as she came, crying out her release with her cheek pressed against mine. I held her like that until she came down, then I managed to work my own pants and boxers down, letting the cooler air caress my heated erection.

The relief was momentary, because she twisted around until she straddled my lap, her hot thighs and pussy enveloping me.

"Who said you could fuck him?" Connor snapped.

"I fucking did," I growled. I wound her hair around my fist and lowered her on to my cock, sliding all the way inside her, my piercings touching her all the way through.

Her eyes widened. "Oh my god," she whispered. "I can feel… Everything. This is… Wow."

"That's the word for it all right." Riley had his pants down, hand wrapped around his length.

Connor turned the phone on him, filming him sliding his fingers up and down his erection.

"Not that I don't appreciate being filmed, but I'd prefer it if you helped me out here." Riley's words were forced out between clenched teeth.

"Let me." Brooks held his hand out for Connor's phone.

I thought Connor might refuse, but he handed it over and knelt down in front of Riley. When Riley's hand dropped away from his cock, Connor replaced it with his own. He stroked him from his balls to his tip before licking him and taking him into his mouth.

"That's so damn hot," Leah whispered.

"You're hot," I said. My hands on her hips, I helped her to rise and fall, slowly riding my cock like she was born to do it. "Your pussy is perfection."

"Your cock is perfection," she said.

"You were made to take it." And I was made to come inside her, which I was going to do faster than I would have liked. I wanted to draw this first time with her out as long as I could, but I'd wanted this moment for too long. I couldn't hold out. I let myself go, grinding up into her as bliss washed over me.

At the same time, she came again, pussy tightening around me, milking me for every drop of pleasure and release. Her head tipped back and she cried out, her voice and mine a harmony.

"Just like that," Brooks said, the phone aimed at her face. At some point, he'd also pushed his pants down and his hand was tight around his base.

Leah kissed me before swinging her leg off me and kneeling beside Brooks. "Do you want to touch each other?" she asked.

Did we? I eyed Brooks' cock, then his face.

He swallowed hard. Turned off the phone and lowered it. "I'd like to," he said tentatively.

Like he was some kind of wild animal, I leaned over slowly and slid the side of my hand up and down his hot length. "I've never touched another guy's dick before." He was a little longer than me, if not quite as thick. Perfect in his own way.

"I like it." Brooks licked his lips.

I wrapped my hand around him firmer and slid it up and down, watching his eyes roll back in his head.

"You're good at that," he told me.

I barked a laugh. "I've had plenty of practice with myself." The only time I'd ever been with anyone else, was in the city, where no questions were asked or given. Just a quick fuck with a random woman for release. It never meant anything, not until now.

Brooks chuckled and rolled his hips, pushing himself deeper between my fingers. Before he could come, I pulled back my hand.

"I don't think you want to come like that." I wasn't ready for anything more, so I helped Leah onto his lap, so she could lower herself onto him the way she had with me.

"This totally works," Brooks said, his voice breaking on the last word.

In the corner of my eye, I watched Riley come, his cock deep in Connor's mouth. Hips jerking, lips parted in orgasm. Connor slid his lips off him, slathering lube onto his rear hole and sliding his cock into Riley's ass, while Riley was draped over the back of an armchair.

"You want to do this someday?" Connor asked between thrusts and glances toward me and Brooks. "He feels so fucking good."

"Someday," was all I could say right now. Watching all that fucking robbed my brain of coherent thought.

Brooks moaned his agreement, and then he was coming inside Leah, his grunts and groans in unison with Connor as he found his release inside Riley.

My eyes were all on Leah as she came for a third time, her breasts bouncing, breaths ragged, cheeks red. In that moment, she was never more beautiful.

Then and there, I fell in love with her.

20

LEAH

I DIDN'T KNOW what time it was. Didn't care. All I knew was the ache in my legs burned like fire. From my toes all the way up my thighs was pure agony. I tried to roll over and whimpered from the pain.

"Leah?" A sleepy voice came from beside me. Riley. He lay on one side of me, Connor on the other. "Are you okay?"

"Yes. No." My eyes were full of hot tears, which leaked down my cheeks, even as I brushed them away.

"Why, what?" The bed moved and the lamp beside it turned on with a click. Riley was looking at me, concern in his blue eyes. "Shit. Flare-up?"

Mutely, I managed to nod.

"What's going on?" Connor rolled over and

rubbed his face. He blinked a couple of times and frowned. "Did you say flare-up? You have something for the pain?"

"On my…" I flapped a hand roughly in the direction of my dresser before drawing back in on myself.

"I'll get it." Riley rolled off the bed, walking naked to the dresser to pick up a bottle of painkillers. He tossed them to Connor and disappeared out the door, coming back a moment later with a glass of water.

"Can you sit up?" Connor tipped a couple of pills onto his palm and closed the bottle again.

I couldn't respond. If I moved, it would hurt. If I lay still, it would hurt. Lying still was the easier of the two.

"Come on, be a good girl and sit up. You need to take these." He placed his hands on my shoulders and gently guided me so I was barely sitting up against the back pillows. Taking the glass from Riley, he lifted it to my lips and waited until I parted them before tipping a little bit of water inside. The pills were next.

"Be a good girl and swallow." He smirked at the innuendo.

I swivelled my gaze toward him, but this was not

the time to be a brat. I swallowed down the pills and lay back down.

"What's wrong?" Brooks appeared in the doorway, Josiah right behind him. There wasn't enough room in the bed for five, so they slept in the spare room. Or at least, they were sleeping. Now, they were both wide awake.

"Flare-up," Riley said, keeping his voice low like he didn't want to disturb me too much. As if he might make the pain worse.

"What can we do?" Josiah hurried in and sat on the side of the bed, careful not to put any weight on me.

"Heat packs," Brooks said. "Where are they?" He glanced around before spotting them on the dresser. He grabbed them up and disappeared out the door. The microwave beeped and started to hum, suggesting he'd put them inside to warm them.

Connor eased the covers off me and moved down to start slowly massaging my feet.

"You don't have to do that," I whispered hoarsely. I felt bad for waking them all up. If they were sleeping in their own houses, this wouldn't have happened. I would have managed to get my painkillers and heat pack. Somehow.

"Yes, we do," Connor said simply. "That's what

we're here for." His hands were magic, soothing my skin and taking some of the edge off the pain.

"Here." Brooks handed the heat packs to Josiah, who placed one to either side of my legs.

"Tell me if that gets too hot," Josiah said. "Or cold. Or..." Out of options, he shrugged.

"It's perfect," I said. Of course Brooks would know exactly how long to put them on for. He'd seen me do it. I hadn't know he'd paid that much attention. Clearly he was attentive in ways I hadn't even noticed. I appreciated it now.

"That's helping?" Riley hovered behind Connor, his cock swinging between his thighs every time he moved.

"It is," I said firmly. "Thank you."

"Ri, go and run a bubble bath," Connor said without glancing over his shoulder.

I opened my mouth to say they didn't have to do that either, but Connor gave me a sharp look until I closed it again.

Riley nodded and hurried out again to the bathroom. The sound of running water filtering through the house a few moments later.

"Hey." Brooks sat down beside my upper body. "I'm sorry I made fun of you with this. It was a bullshit thing to do. That looks painful."

"It is, but this is making it better," I said softly. As painful as it was, being taken care of by four incredible men was easing the agony. And reminding me I was cared about.

"You must be cold." He pulled the covers around me, wrapping me up as best he could without getting in the way of Connor and his massaging hands.

"Do you want some tea?" Josiah asked.

"I don't want to be a bother, but I'd love some," I said tentatively. "Thank you."

He nodded, rose and went into the kitchen. As the water started to boil, the sound of water passing through the pipes stopped.

"Bath is ready." Riley appeared in the doorway again.

"Help me get her up," he said.

While Brooks and Riley peeled off the covers again, Connor scooped me up in his arms and carried me all the way to the bath before lowering me under the water. From the smirk on his face, he was remembering the time he made me beg for his help. He must have realised how much pain I was in, because he didn't do it this time. He lifted his arms away and let me sink under the delicious warmth.

"Thank you," I said on a sigh. "This feels good." As good as I could feel with the ache still persisting. It wasn't as bad as it had been. The pain was almost bearable now.

Riley crouched down behind the bath and started to wet my hair before grabbing the shampoo and squeezing some of it onto his hand. Gently and carefully, he started to massage it into my scalp, his hands like a different kind of magic on my skin.

I closed my eyes and let him work while the warmth of the water seeped into my bones.

"Can you lower your head so I can rinse it off?" he asked softly.

I murmured my agreement and tilted my head back so my hair was under the water. He worked his fingers through until all of the shampoo was gone, then grabbed a washcloth to wash my back and my upper body.

After a moment, Brooks picked up another washcloth and started on my feet and legs.

"I feel very spoilt," I said without opening my eyes.

"You could never be spoiled," Riley said.

"Don't bet on it," Brooks teased.

I opened one eye to glare at him playfully. He just grinned back at me and went on washing.

"Such a brat." I closed my eye.

"It's part of my charm." He laughed.

"Are you okay?" Josiah crouched between the other guys. I opened my eyes as he offered me a cup of tea.

"Better than I was, thank you," I said. I accepted the cup and took a sip. "The only thing that's missing are peeled grapes."

"Fuck," Connor swore. "We're out of grapes. If I knew we'd need them, I would have ordered some." For a moment I thought he was serious, but then he gave the slightest hint of a smile.

"They're not exactly in season," I said. "I prefer them in liquid form anyway."

"I can get you some ice cream if you want?" Riley asked. "There's some left over from dinner."

"That's sweet of you, but I'm still digesting," I said. "What's the time?"

"About two o'clock in the morning." It was Connor who answered.

"You have to be at work in a few hours," I said. I really had disrupted everything, hadn't I?

"We'll be fine," he said. "You're what's important right now."

"That's sweet of you," I said.

Josiah smirked.

Connor caught the expression on his face and rolled his eyes. "Yeah, yeah. Put it on the calendar.

Connor Ferguson was sweet. First and last time ever."

"You've been sweet before," Riley said. "I bet you anything you'll be sweet again."

"If you keep pointing it out, I'll make it my life's work never to be sweet," Connor said.

We all laughed at that, none of us believing a word of it. Like it or not, he was who he was.

I closed my eyes again and listened to the guys go on about this and, only hearing half of it. I sipped my tea until it was done and Josiah took the cup out of my hand.

"Are you ready to get out of the bath yet?" he asked.

"I probably should, before I start to get wrinkly," I said with some reluctance. It was comfortable in there, but the water has started to cool and I was getting sleepy again. I needed to get back to sleep and so did they.

"We don't mind if you get wrinkles," Riley said. But he kissed the top of my wet head and stood to get a towel to wrap around me after the others helped me out.

"Can you stand okay?" Connor asked, his brow wrinkled adorably with worry.

"I'm fine," I said. "If I'm not, I have four of you to catch me."

"Yes, you do," Riley said, towelling me dry quickly before wrapping the towel around my hair. He barely finished doing that before he was scooping me up in his arms and carrying me back to bed. "You smell amazing. Like lavender and vanilla. Ironic, since you're anything but vanilla."

I stifled a yawn with my fist. "I feel nice and clean and… Relaxed." The ache was a lot duller now, tolerable. Just.

"We should have fucked you gentler," Josiah said with regret.

"It was perfect," I assured him. "If it wasn't, I would have said so."

Okay, riding their laps the way I had was probably not the best idea. At the time, I was enjoying myself. Living in the moment. Now I was paying for it.

Still, I couldn't bring myself to feel too badly about it. If I did, it might stop me from living life, and fucking, the way I wanted to. No, I wasn't going to let this set me back.

"You fucking better," Connor said. "I'm not having you in pain because you're too stubborn to speak up. When you feel better, I'm going to smack your ass as a reminder."

Yes, please.

He narrowed his eyes, but he'd love it as much as I would.

I knew from experience, the next couple of days were going to be uncomfortable, but hopefully I was passed the worst of it. This time. Next time, I might be alone. Sure, Brooks was living here now, but he'd be working a lot of late nights at the pub.

As if he read my mind, Connor said, "You should move in with us. Make sure someone is always around if you need anything."

"What he said," Riley agreed.

Josiah looked as though he was thinking along the same lines, but up at his cottage, rather than here in town. He might always feel out of place here compared to up there. Not surprising, given everything that happened in the last twenty years. I didn't expect him to give up everything for me. That whole conversation was for later.

One way or another, we'd figure things out.

"She wasn't alone," Brooks said, giving them all the side eye. "I would have taken care of her."

"What if you weren't here?" Connor asked. "This needs to happen." At least for tonight, no one else had any more argument against the idea. Including me.

"I'll think about it," I said sleepily as Riley lay me down in the centre of the bed. That was a problem for future me. Something I'd think about in the morning. Or should I say, when the sun was up.

I was vaguely aware of one of them lying to either side of me before I was asleep again.

2 1

LEAH

A TAP at the door roused me from a doze. It creaked open slowly and Whitney's face appeared in the gap.

"Hey." Her voice was soft, more tentative than usual. "Can we come in?"

"Um, yeah." I wiped hair off the side of my face and grimaced at the drool on my cheek. I must have been deeper asleep than I realised. "Hi."

She pushed the door open all the way and stepped in, followed by Fiona, Holly and Fiona's daughter, Sarah. Each carried a bag or covered tray.

"Connor said you had a bad flare-up and may need a bit of help." Whitney carried her tray to the kitchen and placed it on the bench. "He's caught up at the moment, after last night's snowfall."

I caught sight of it out the window, but mostly I'd

spent the day on the couch with heat packs and painkillers, reading on my e-reader.

"That's sweet of him," I said.

"Riley texted me and said you'd need help," Fiona said. She placed a bag down in front of me and opened it to pull out some bath bombs, chocolate and a couple of candles.

"I brought you a blanket my grandma made." Sarah, suddenly looking shy, handed me a beautifully crocheted blanket in shades of blue and green.

"It's beautiful," I said, holding it up in front of me before draping it over my legs. "Thank you so much. And please tell your grandmother I said thank you."

I hadn't expected any of this. Leave it to the guys to make sure I was taken care of, even when they weren't here. I brushed away a tear and smiled back at Sarah, who looked pleased.

"This is from all of us." Holly placed a plate of cookies on the table in front of me, and took another tray into the kitchen. "Snack for now and dinner for later."

"You girls are the best," I said, wiping away another tear.

"Did we make you sad?" Sarah looked worried.

"No, you made me super happy," I assured her. "It's nice of you to take care of me like this."

"It's our pleasure." Whitney put on the coffee maker and came to sit down near me. She held the plate of cookies so I could take one, then snagged one for herself. "Besides, Connor was very insistent." She grinned and took a bite.

"He usually is." I bit into my cookie, enjoying the explosion of chocolate chips on my tongue.

"More so than usual. He's got it bad for you, girl." She hummed her appreciation of the cookie. "So good."

"Do you mind?" I asked. "Me and Connor, I mean."

"And Riley, and Brooks, and Josiah," Holly said with a teasing smile.

My face heated. "Well, yeah. But none of you are related to them." I paused for a moment before adding, "That I know of anyway."

"Riley is my cousin," Holly said. "I don't care what you and he do. As long as he doesn't do anything to hurt you. Otherwise my brothers might have words to say with him." Judging by the expression on her face, they wouldn't be gentle about it.

"I think Riley would hurt himself before he hurt Leah," Fiona said. "He's just as gone as Connor."

"They're just as gone for each other," Whitney said. "And to answer your question, no, I don't mind.

In fact, I'm happy for all of you. I never thought I'd see my brother settle down, even with Riley. Those two are wild together, but since you've been in the picture, it's like..." She thought for a moment. "Like the last piece of the puzzle is in place. Fuck, that sounds corny." She tipped her head back and laughed.

"It's true though," Holly said. "I feel that way with the four of us too. Sorry, I mean the five of us," she said with a laugh when Sarah started to protest. "Not that things weren't amazing before that, but I like having you around."

"I like having her around too," Sarah said loudly. "I'm going to be an artist, like Leah. Can you teach me to draw and paint like you do?"

"I'd be happy to," I said. I meant it. The kid was cute and I was always happy to foster creativity.

"When Leah is feeling better," Fiona gently reminded her daughter. "She needs to rest right now, not work."

"Does she have a migraine?" Sarah scrunched up her brow. "Mommy gets migraines sometimes and she has to lie down in the dark. I sit and draw, but sometimes I make a grilled cheese for her to eat for dinner."

"You do a good job taking care of her," I said. I

quickly explained about my arthritis, while she wrinkled her nose in sympathy.

"I don't want to have that," she declared. "Or migraines."

"Me either," Fiona said ruefully.

I could tell what she was thinking, but no one was going to tell Sarah migraines tended to be hereditary. Hopefully she wouldn't find out the hard way. If she did, at least she knew how to take care of herself. Yeah, small mercy, I know.

"Sometimes not very nice things happen to nice people," Whitney said in her teacher voice. "That's when we know who we can rely on to help us when we need help. That's also when we know how tough we can be. If I had arthritis or migraines, I'd be crying in a corner. But your mommy, and Leah, they're super tough." She leaned in and loudly whispered to Sarah, "They might be superheroes."

Fiona barked a laugh, but Sarah turned adoring eyes to her. I suspected she already thought her mother was a superhero. Or at least a badass.

As for me, I didn't feel much like either of those things.

"I used to be a sculptor," I blurted out. "I was starting to get noticed. People were asking for my work. Paying for it." Paying well. "When I couldn't do it anymore, I didn't feel tough at all. Instead, I ran away and came here."

I brushed tears off my cheeks again. What was wrong with me today? I was a blubbering mess. Pain and broken sleep would do that to anyone, I supposed. I was only human after all.

Whitney scooted over and put an arm around me. "Don't think of it as running away. You reinvented yourself. You went from being a sculptor in the city to being a different kind of artist, in a small town. Can you honestly say you miss that life?" She drew her head back and gave me a steady look, silently insisting on my honesty, at least with myself. Sometimes, she and her brother weren't that different.

"I…" Could I? "I never thought about it like that. I guess I don't." If it wasn't for the flare-ups, I wouldn't have come here. Or I might, but would I have stayed? I would have had a life to return to. I could live without the pain, but what about the rest of it? I would have missed my four guys and my three… Four best friends.

When I really thought about it, I was lucky. If I hadn't stuck around, I never would have known about Coral Clarke. I might have spent the rest of my life oblivious to the past.

"Of course you don't," Fiona said. "Living in Aurora Hollow is peak life. No pun intended. And if you ask me anything, people should be paying a crap ton for your paintings and drawings. Once people realise you're here, they'll be lining up all the way down to the bottom of the mountain to buy one."

"They'll have to get into the queue behind us," Holly said. She nodded like the matter was settled.

Of course, I didn't expect any of them to actually buy anything from me. Their words, their support, it meant more to me than any dollar amount.

"Damn straight they will," Whitney agreed. "Although I might have to start saving now for the three million dollar paintings."

"The day anyone pays that much for a work of mine," I said disbelievingly.

"They'll be getting a bargain," Holly said firmly.

"I don't know about that," I said modestly. If I could sell a few for a fraction of that, I'd be able to buy a place. Maybe somewhere big enough for five people. With space for Josiah to be alone if he needed it. And for me to make my art.

"Three million dollars?" Sarah's eyes were huge.

"People can pay a lot for art," Whitney told her.

"Mommy..." Sarah gave Fiona a sly look.

"As much as I'd love to pay three million dollars

for your art so I can put it on the fridge, I don't have that kind of money." Fiona shook her head and laughed.

If she did have that kind of money, no doubt she'd pay for the privilege of displaying Sarah's work. I wished my mother had the same attitude as she did. Sarah was a lucky kid. Was I too old for Fiona to adopt me? I mentally laughed at myself for the silly idea.

"Awww." But Sarah was still smiling, her mind ticking over. Like she was trying to figure out who might have money for her work. Hopefully when she figured it out, she'd tell me so I could sell to them too.

"In the meantime, it'll be Halloween in a couple of days," Holly said. "Will you be up to joining in?" She adjusted her blonde ponytail, and looked concerned like she didn't want me to push myself too hard just to make them happy.

"I hope so," I said sincerely. "I've been looking forward to it. I have a feeling the guys are planning something, but I don't know what."

"I don't think I've ever seen a pair of adult men more excited over a holiday than Connor and Riley," Whitney said. "I think they like to channel their inner serial killer, stalker or whatever costume they decide on." She smiled indulgently, as if they were a pair of little boys, not a couple of grown men. Of course, as Connor's older sister, she probably thought of them as little boys. Didn't big sisters always feel that way? Especially when the brothers were like those two.

"That sounds like them," I agreed. Brooks too. Although, since he tracked my car and set up a camera to watch me, did he need to channel his inner stalker, or had he done that already? At some point, I'd need to sit down with him and find out if he did anything else. I wouldn't be surprised if he had candid photos of me on his phone. If it was anyone else, I'd be horrified. Brooks, though, was mostly harmless.

As far as I knew.

"You should be getting your results back a few days after that," Fiona said softly. She glanced at Sarah to indicate she hadn't said anything about it to her daughter. That was fortunate, the situation was strange enough without involving a kid. At some point, she probably have to be told, but for now it was better that she wasn't.

"Hopefully," I said. Honestly, I was trying not to think about it too much myself. Worrying about it wouldn't bring them any sooner. It wouldn't change the result. It would mean I'd have to confront my mother sooner rather than later. In the meantime, I could live one day after the other and let the future take care of itself when it came. Not to mention, I wanted to enjoy Halloween first. My first holiday in Aurora Hollow.

"So, what are you going as?" Holly asked brightly. They started talking about their costumes, and sharing ideas while I sat back and slowly nibbled on another cookie.

22

BROOKS

"You have to be kidding me." I stared at the costume Connor held in his hand.

"I think it's kinda cool," Riley said, giving me a frowning glance.

"Cool?" I echoed. "It's fucking epic." Hating that it was Connor who came up with this idea, I took the black and silver mask out of Conner's fingers and gave it a closer look. It looked vaguely like a skull, if the skull had shattered into a hundred pieces. It was violent and beautiful at the same time.

"It's very you," Connor said as I held it up in front of my face. "You have a black hoodie and black jeans?"

My voice muffled by the mask, I said, "Of course

I do. So we're all dressing like that? All black, and with masks."

"Yeah. Like all those social media videos," Connor said. "Masked men hunting our woman. I have the perfect outfit for Leah too."

"Genius," Riley said. He was looking down at his own mask. His was black and red, also the look of a shattered skull, but with fewer fragments. Connor's had more fragments than mine, but his was black and gold.

"Did you bring one for Josiah?" I asked. Between work here at the pub and him living where he did, I hadn't seen him for a couple of days. With any luck, I didn't sound like I was too eager for his company. I was trying to play it cool.

"Duh." From under his mask, Connor pulled out one that was completely black. The shattered effect was still there, but only if you saw it in the right light.

"You think he'll wear it?" I asked. Josiah was just as likely to tell Connor to shove it up his ass.

"He'll wear it," Connor said with certainty. "He'll want to do this for Leah. She's going to love it."

"Speaking of Josiah." Riley nodded toward the door leading into the pub.

I looked over as he stepped inside and gave us all

a dubious look. As if he thought we were plotting against him. His face was all hard lines and angles, covered with stubble like he hadn't shaved for several days.

I couldn't help it, I dug the dark, brooding thing he had going on. At the same time, it was conflicting. Before him, I never met a man I wanted to fuck. Not that I'd admit to myself anyway. Like any normal guy, I fixated on movie stars and rock stars, but I hadn't let myself think about men in real, day-to-day life. I had my share of hookups with women, and was never disappointed, but this was a whole perspective shift. Between him and Leah, I might not look at another person for as long as I lived. Not like that, anyway.

The city version of me would have hated myself, but the guy I was becoming was here for it.

"Hey," Josiah said with a grunt. He stepped over like he wasn't sure if he should turn and walk back out again, or stick around and join in. The fact he was here at all seemed like a big deal to me. I knew it'd be a big deal to Leah.

"Connor has a present for you." Riley held out the mask to Josiah, while putting his own in front of his face. "We all got one."

"Is this Connor's way of saying we're all ugly as

shit?" Josiah asked. He took the mask and examined it closely. His fingers tracing a line from the top of it, down to the jaw. Appreciating the texture and subtle design. I suspected he would have given any of the others back, but this one was perfect for him. A dark mask to hide his usual dark mask. What was underneath all those layers? Not someone who'd ever be light-hearted, that was certain. But maybe we'd be able to get him to relax and show the real him to us. And to himself.

"Exactly," Connor said sarcastically. "We're too hideous to be seen."

"Speak for yourself." Riley lowered his mask. "It's almost a crime to cover this face, but I'll do it for Leah."

"Of course you will," I said. "This is going to blow her mind."

"I predict lots of blowing in our future," Riley said with a nod.

"If you keep saying that, I'm going to make you blow me right here," Connor growled.

Riley leaned over to me and loudly whispered, "He says that like he thinks I wouldn't."

I shrugged. "The place is closed." The door was unlocked because we anticipated Josiah, but everyone in town would be getting ready for

Halloween. The pub was hosting a party, but Jacob gave me the night off to enjoy the holiday. I suspected that was Connor's doing, but I wasn't going to ask.

Connor tilted his chin up and regarded Riley for a moment. "We need to get changed and get to Leah's. You can suck me off there."

Riley gave him a salute. "Yes, sir." If he was disappointed, he didn't let on.

"Change?" Josiah asked. I'd forgotten he missed that part of the conversation.

"You look perfect," I said. I realised what I said and blinked a couple of times, trying to stop myself from looking like an idiot. "I mean, you're already dressed all in black. That was the plan here."

"Right," he said simply. I got the impression he saw straight through me, but he wasn't going to call me out. Not yet.

"Let's get out of here then," Connor said. "We have a woman to stalk."

"That sounds so messed up," Riley said, grinning.

"You can always sit it out," I suggested, expecting him to decline the kind offer.

Predictably, he laughed. "No chance." He slipped out the door behind Connor.

I gestured for Josiah to follow him so I could lock

the door behind us. Also predictably, Connor checked to make sure I did it right. As if turning a lock was beyond me.

Asshole.

I smirked at him, but his only response was to turn away and start down the sidewalk which was cleared of snow an hour or so ago. None fell since, leaving it good to walk on, for now. If *fucking cold* could be considered good. It even smelled like cold. Although, this afternoon it was balanced with a smell of spices coming from the Snowdrop Café and the bakery on the corner. Smells of Halloween. The scent of warm fires and carving pumpkins.

We made our way past the house Gavin Clarke lived in. I'd been filled in on him and his role in town almost as soon as I arrived. I felt sorry for him, but it was weird to think he might be Leah's father. That whole situation was all sorts of fucked up. I hated what it was doing to Leah, and I hated myself for being an asshole to her since we met.

There was nothing I could do about the past, but I could treat her better now. Maybe. Both of us enjoyed giving each other shit. Why stop now? I might dial it back a little, but that was all.

"Did you happen to see the people who took her?" I asked as I walked beside Josiah.

Were they people she'd recognised? People who were in her life now, like her mother. Like, a small voice said to me, my father. They said they hadn't met until years later, but was that true? If my father knew what happened to her all this time...

"It's hazy," Josiah said, his voice low so only I could hear. "Mostly I was looking at her."

"Is there any chance one was a woman?" I asked.

He glanced at me. "I've gone over and over it in my head, and I don't remember. I just remember a dark car and her looking scared. One of them wore a dark jacket. Black, or dark blue." He shook his head. "I've been trying to forget about it for twenty years. Now I'm trying to think back and it's a blur. I wish I remembered more." He seemed regretful. His eyes troubled.

"It was a long time ago," I said. "No one expects you to have everything locked into your brain."

Connor looked over his shoulder at us, the dip of his brows suggesting he disagreed.

"No one," I said firmly. "None of us remembers every detail of everything twenty years ago." I barely remembered my mother, who died about the same time Coral Clarke disappeared. My father remarried a couple of years later, but that ended in divorce a decade ago. Lucky for everyone concerned. If I heard another fight between them, I might have throttled them both. Felicity Kent was a better match for him than her. As much as anyone could be a good match for a grumpy, self-obsessed asshole like my father. Yeah, I know, the apple didn't fall far from the tree.

"Yeah." But Josiah didn't seem convinced. Of course not, he'd spent all that time beating himself up. That was going to be a difficult habit for him to break. I hoped he'd be able to.

I hoped I'd be able to help him. Would he even let me? Honestly, the real question here was, could he stop me? Leah and I might not be related, but we shared a stubborn streak. I couldn't remember a time either of us backed down from anything.

I glanced back at Gavin Clarke's house to see someone watching from the front window. He didn't move. I couldn't tell if he even blinked. He just stared at us for the longest time before the curtain dropped back into place, hiding him from view.

"That was strange," I said.

Josiah sighed. "Not for me. We haven't spoken to each other for twenty years, but whenever we're around each other, one of us will stop and stare. Sometimes I feel like I should try to say something, but then I don't know what. Sorry, I suppose." He dropped his gaze toward the sidewalk.

"I'm no expert, but you could start with hello," I suggested. "Or wait for those DNA results." They'd have plenty to talk about then. Amends to make. If that was possible.

"Yeah," he said softly. "There's still a chance…" He didn't elaborate and I didn't ask. We all knew what the possibilities were and that whatever happened, there'd be more questions. Hopefully some of them had answers to go with them.

I was half tempted to contact my father or my stepmother and ask them myself, but not only would that piss Leah off, they were her questions to ask. She'd want to see them face-to-face, to see the expression on their faces and hear what they had to say.

I won't say I wasn't tempted to do it anyway, because she and I had an antagonistic relationship for so long it was a difficult habit to break. We enjoyed getting a rise out of each other, but that would be a few steps too far, even for me.

Of course, even knowing that boundary, I still wanted to push it.

It seemed as though both Josiah and I had some

work to do on ourselves. Admitting it was the first step, right?

"What the hell?" Connor's irritated words broke through my thoughts. "What are they doing there?"

"Good question," Riley sounded just as annoyed. His voice held a darker tone than I'd heard from him before. Whatever was going on, it sounded like he was ready to start throwing punches.

I tried not to think too much about how hot it was. Violence wasn't supposed to be attractive, but with these guys, it was scalding hot. Every word made me want to peel off my skin and crawl under theirs.

"Fuck," Josiah said, ducking his head.

"What is it?" I said, confused. We were a handful of steps from Leah's house. The door was open and she stood just inside, talking to two men I recognised. My new boss, Jacob Ferguson, and Riley's father, Henry.

What the hell were they doing here?

23

LEAH

"THINK ABOUT WHAT WE SAID, OKAY?" Jacob Ferguson wasn't quite as forceful at getting his opinion across as his son, but he expected to be obeyed.

"Yeah, I'll think about it," I said, if only to appease them so they'd leave. This whole conversation was uncomfortable. In the corner of my eye, I saw the guys approaching. Each looked less impressed than the last. Josiah hung back, while Connor and Riley strode toward us.

"Is there a problem?" Connor's jaw was tight.

"No problem, son," Jacob said. "Just having a little chat with Miss Kent." He patted his son's shoulder before nodding to Henry. "We should get going, we have plenty to do." He gave Josiah openly hostile look before stalking past, in the direction of the pub.

"Dad," Riley started.

"Like he said, we have plenty to do," Henry said. "I'll see you at the shindig?"

"Are you a hundred years old?" Riley asked, his tone lighter than the look in his eyes. If he thought something was going on, he wouldn't hesitate to act on it. He still wasn't sure if he shouldn't, if the doubtful look he gave his father was an indication.

Henry laughed. "It feels like it sometimes. You lot stay out of trouble, okay?" He also glanced at Josiah before heading off down the street.

"What the hell was that about?" Connor demanded as he herded all of us inside.

Josiah hesitated, his hands pressed close to himself, but he followed anyway.

I rubbed the heel of my hand across my forehead. "They came to warn me about spending time with all of you. Apparently people are talking."

"Fuck people," Riley spat. "I should have—" He turned away and stepped towards the door.

It was Connor who grabbed his arm and stopped him. "What are you going to do? Strangle your father and bury him in a bank of snow?"

"If I have to." But Riley sagged and ran a hand over the back of his neck. "Where does he get off?"

"The same place my father does," Connor said darkly. "What else did they say?"

"They told her to stay away from me," Josiah said.

I wished I could tell him he was wrong, but he wasn't. "Yeah, they said that too, but they also hinted that people were worried I was dating Brooks as well."

"Because you are," Brooks said. "I don't give a shit what they think."

"Even if you lose your job?" I asked.

"I'll get another one. I'm not giving you up for anything." Brooks placed a hand on my hip and pulled me to him.

"He won't fire you," Connor said. "I won't let him. I'll talk to him. Tell him to mind his own fucking business."

"I'll do the same with my father," Riley said.

"I don't want to cause problems with your families," I said.

"You didn't." Connor placed his hands on my cheeks, almost hitting Brooks in the face. "They did that. They're small town, mountain men with small town, mountain men ideas. It's time they caught up with the rest of the world." He pressed his forehead to mine. "Okay?"

"Okay," I whispered.

"If it makes you feel any better, my father is a hypocrite," Connor said. "I know for a fact he's been unfaithful to my mother. But this—" He lifted his head and glanced around. "None of us is going behind anyone else's back. If he wants to throw stones, he should throw them at himself."

Riley made a confused sound at the back of his throat. "Do you think my father is projecting?"

"I think my father dragged him into this," Connor told him. "I wouldn't be surprised if they were the only ones who had any problem with this situation. No one else seems to give a crap."

I thought about that for a moment. "Right. Everyone else has been lovely." At least, they were to my face.

"Everyone else loves you almost as much as we do," Riley said. "I think we should get ready for the party and go down there and show our fathers we won't be intimidated."

"That's exactly what we're doing." Connor had a bag dangling from his arm. He reached into it, his eyes on me. He handed me a white dress with long sleeves. "I brought your costume."

I took the dress and shook it out. It fell to just above my knees, the skirt flaring out.

"Go and put it on," he said. He exchanged cagey looks with the other guys, so I knew something was up, but I wasn't sure what yet.

"Okay," I said slowly. "I'll be right back." I disappeared into my bedroom, deliberately closing the door behind me. I stripped down to my underwear, before putting the dress over my head and tugging it down into place. A glance at my reflection in the mirror showed an almost innocent looking version of myself. A woman waiting for four bad boys to corrupt her. Or maybe she wasn't so innocent and she was waiting to corrupt them.

Either way, I grabbed a jacket, slipped my feet into boots and stepped back out of the bedroom.

I let out a squeak of surprise, seeing four men dressed entirely in black, their faces covered in masks.

"I've just stepped into a video." I looked from one to the other, taking in the different details on their masks. Silver, red, gold and black. Mysterious, and hot enough to melt my panties.

"Is this where I start running?" I asked. It might be worth enduring a flare-up.

"After the party," Connor promised. "We have some business to take care of first. We'll show them we're together and we won't be messed with. Then we'll come back here and mess around." Speaking so firmly, with the mask over his face, made my nipples tighten.

These men were a pure fantasy come to life and they were all mine.

"Okay, but no throwing anyone into a snow bank," I said.

"I make no promises," Riley said. "If I do it, no one will know it's me with this on." He gestured at his mask.

"Except us," Brooks said.

"Yeah, but you're not going to say anything," Riley said. "Don't tell me you wouldn't help dispose of the evidence."

"I could be convinced," Brooks said.

"If those masks are going to turn you into homicidal maniacs…" I started.

"We should wear them more often?" Riley suggested.

"That wasn't where I was going with that." I shrugged into my jacket and grabbed up my bag and phone.

"Of course it was." Brooks placed his hands on my shoulders and ran the pad of his thumbs over the back of my neck. "What girl doesn't want four masked, homicidal maniac boyfriends? I've seen you read plenty of books like that before."

"There's a difference between book boyfriends and real boyfriends," I pointed out.

"Yeah, real boyfriends are real," Riley said. He took my hand and pulled me towards the door and out onto the street. "Real boyfriends look after you when you need them to. And real boyfriends stand up for you when their fathers decide to be dickheads."

"Exactly," Connor agreed. He took my other hand and we walked side by side in a line, all the way to the pub. We stepped through the door together, Brooks and Josiah shuffling so we'd all fit.

The place was warm and packed, smelling of wood smoke and bourbon. Everyone in the place was wearing a costume, some with masks, many without.

I half expected silence to fall when we appeared, but all we got were a few glances and greetings before everyone went back to chatting and drinking.

"See, no one cares," Riley said. "Except them." He nodded to where Jacob and Henry stood beside the bar. They didn't seem to have noticed our arrival. Not until Connor marched up and tapped his father on the shoulder. He pushed his mask up to the top of his face, so his anger was visible.

"Ah, you made it." Jacob's smile didn't meet his eyes. They narrowed when he looked at me, then took in each of the guys one after the other.

"Where else would we be?" Connor asked. "This is the party of the year. Of course we'd bring our girlfriend here." His voice was laced with barely controlled fury.

"Our…" Jacob sighed as though he was frustrated at dealing with a child. "Connor, I know you think—"

"You have no idea what I think," Connor snapped. "This is how it is, whether you like it or not. What exactly is your problem anyway?"

Jacob's face turned red. "Don't take that tone with me. I just want what's best for my boy."

"I'm not a boy anymore," Connor said. He opened his mouth to say something else, but shook his head. "You know what, I'm not having this conversation. This is my life and this is how I'm living it. With Leah, Riley, Brooks and, yes, with Josiah. Whether you like it or not."

"I should have insisted you take over this place," Jacob said. "It's past time you stopped playing around. Grow up and do a real man's job."

All of us were silent while those words sunk in. None of us quite believing what we were hearing. All of us tense we waited for Connor's response.

"Running my own business is a real man's job," Connor said coldly. "This place is your dream, not mine."

"Life is more than dreams," Jacob said. "You need to wake up to reality. Do you really think you can have a relationship with a woman who's involved with three other boys?"

"No," Connor said. He lifted his chin and stared his father down. Completely unflinching. Unbending.

My heart skipped a beat. For a moment I was confused, then Connor spoke again.

"I can have a relationship with a woman who is involved with three other *men*. Look at us, Dad. Do any of us look like a boy?" Dressed all in black, even with a mask on top of his head, there was nothing boyish about Connor Ferguson.

Thankfully he'd chosen that costume and not something frivolous, like Mickey Mouse. That would have made this whole argument a lot less convincing.

"You should both calm down," Henry said, stepping between them. "Connor, you know this isn't good for your father's heart." He raised his hands to either side, trying to placate both men.

He looked like an older version of Riley. Of all the guys, he was the one most likely to laugh and crack jokes to break the tension, rather than swinging punches. I suspected those would be a last resort, but by no means off the table.

Honestly, I wasn't sure he was completely joking about the snow bank thing. Only as a last resort though. Hopefully, it was no resort at all, not really. I didn't want to be an accessory to murder.

Connor grunted. "He should have thought of that before he picked this fight. But you know what, I'm ending it. This isn't about Leah, it's about me taking over the Frosty Brew. Correction, me *not* taking it over. I'm going to live my life, not his." He started to turn away.

"Maybe I should leave the place to your sister," Jacob said.

Connor turned back. He spread his hands to either side. "Be my guest." He slammed his mask back over his face and stalked away.

I gave both Jacob and Henry a long look and a tentative smile before I followed Connor into the crowds.

I didn't want to be the cause of any friction, but I

got the impression that existed long before I was on the scene. I knew Connor loved his father, but he wasn't giving up the business he was building with Riley. I hoped, in time, Jacob would accept that. And accept me in his son's life.

24

LEAH

WE STAYED at the party for around an hour while Connor seethed. Every so often, he glanced in his father's direction, eyes snapping. I managed to fit in a quick conversation with Whitney and Holly before Riley grabbed my hand.

"Let's get out of here," he said over the music. "Before Connor breaks an eyeball glaring at Jacob."

"Whose eyeball?" I asked but I let him drag me to the door.

"I was thinking his, but now you mention it..." Riley laughed.

The other three stood by the door, finishing off their drinks and placing their glasses down on a nearby table.

"Someone mentioned chasing you?" Brooks pushed his mask high enough to show me his grin.

"I don't know if that's a good—" I squealed as Riley ducked and picked me up, leaving me draped over his shoulder.

"No problem," he shouted and started out the door at a run. His arm was secure over my legs to keep me from jostling to much.

I laughed and watched the sidewalk blur as we raced down the street. "You're out of your mind!" I lifted my head to see the other three jogging along behind, exactly like something out of a video. No rushing, just following. Knowing they were going to catch their prey and eat their fill.

At the end of the block, Riley slowed to a stop, carefully carrying me over the road to the other side. The other three slowed as well, stalking, their hands at their sides.

"Are you wet?" Riley asked.

"I've been wet for the last hour or two," I said. "Ever since I saw you with those masks on."

"I might never take mine off then," he said with a playful growl.

"I wouldn't be able to see your face if you don't." I put a pout in my tone.

"Awww, you like my face?" He glanced at me over his shoulder.

"I love your face," I said. "But aren't you supposed to be a crazed stalker right now?"

"I'm definitely crazed," he said with a chuckle. "Right now, I'm trying to work out if I can get into your place and lock the others out for the rest of the night. Then I can take my time licking every single centimetre of you, making you scream six or seven times."

My throbbing clit liked the idea, but I suspected the other three men would not.

"Connor would break a window to get in," I said.

"I knew he was an asshole." Riley exhaled as though he was actually frustrated. "I should have taken you out the back door of the pub. We could have had a head start to a place I know near the top of the mountain. A little cabin. We could spend all night fucking in front of the fire."

"We can hear you, you know," Connor called out.

Riley flipped him off over his opposite shoulder. "We don't care."

"You will when we tie you down and force you to watch us fuck her," Connor said.

"I can't decide if that's a threat or a promise," Riley said.

"Both." Connor stepped past us to the front door of my place, sliding his key into the lock.

"Nothing says badass, crazed stalker maniac like a front door key," Riley said with a laugh.

Connor grunted. "Even maniacs use keys. How the fuck else are we going to get inside?"

"We could have broken the door down, but that would let the cold air in," Brooks said, shivering.

"Don't damage a perfectly good door." Josiah stepped past everyone to the wood stove and opened it to add a few more logs.

"If you're not careful you're going to have to hand over your asshole card," Riley said to all of them.

"Including you," Connor told him.

"Bullshit, I was the one who abducted the damsel." Riley patted my ass.

"Only because you thought of it before I did," Connor said. He kicked the door shut behind us. It closed with a thud before he carefully locked it.

Riley hummed. "So what you're saying is I'm the smart, badass, crazed stalker maniac."

"Would anyone like some coffee?" I asked, kicking my feet lightly. When they all turned to stare at me, I grinned. "It seemed like the thing to offer." They looked the part, but they'd have to work on the crazed maniac persona for next Halloween.

"There's only one thing I want." Riley marched into my bedroom and lay me down in the middle of the bed. He hesitated. "Fuck."

I looked up at him and let my brow scrunch. "What is it? Is something wrong?"

I glanced around, but as far as I could tell, the place wasn't on fire. No one was knocking at the door. The front of Riley's jeans were tented, so there wasn't a problem there.

"I can't eat you out with this on." I could almost hear his grimace behind the mask. "But I still have fingers." He pushed my dress up to my waist and tugged my panties aside. Eyes peering out from the holes in the mask, he rubbed his thumb around my clit before sliding a finger inside me.

I shivered at his touch, and the sight of the other three men, still masked, gathered around me. My mouth watered when they started to shed their clothes. They held the masks in place so they didn't come off with their hoodies. A minute or two later, I was surrounded by naked, muscular flesh, their cocks jutting out, pointing at me.

"Her mouth isn't covered." Brooks knelt beside me and stroked the tip of his cock across my lips, painting them with his pre-cum.

I licked them, appreciating the salty taste before I

opened and let him slide inside. He groaned softly in appreciation before slowly moving, sliding out and all the way back into the back of my throat.

"So fucking perfect," he whispered. "I love having my stepsister's mouth on my cock. You like that don't you? Your stepbrother fucking your mouth."

I looked up at him and let my smile reach my eyes in response. His special brand of dirty talk was arousing as hell. Making this sound like something more illicit than it really was. Taboo, almost. It got us both going. Driving me closer and closer to the steepest cliff that I was ready to drop off, into nothingness. Knowing they'd be there to catch me when I fell.

I had to pull away from Brooks' cock for a few moments while I came, my body engulfed in an orgasm that had me crying out already. I was barely down when Riley was pulling off the rest of my clothes and lying over me, holding my wrists above my head. He nudged my legs apart with his knees and pushed his cock inside me.

Connor pulled out the lube from the drawer beside the bed and knelt behind Riley, smearing a generous finger full on his rear hole. He tossed the tube aside before pushing himself into Riley's ass, driving him deeper inside me.

All three of us groaned in unison. We lay there like that for a few moments before Connor started to thrust, setting the speed for Riley and me. It took a moment for me to get the rhythm right with rolls of my hips. Then all three of us were moving in harmony, giving and receiving pleasure, filling each other and being filled.

"Fuck, that feels good," Riley whispered. "I might be glad I didn't steal you away to that cabin." He moaned, breathing frantically out from between pursed lips. Fucking while being fucked. Careful in his movements so he didn't dislodge himself or Connor's cock.

"Of course you are," Connor said without breaking rhythm.

Beside us, Brooks and Josiah exchanged looks before, to my surprise, Brooks pulled his cock out of my mouth and dropped to his knees, his hand wrapped around Josiah's length. Then his mouth, his mask dropped onto the floor.

Josiah's whole body stiffened, but then he relaxed and tangled his fingers in Brooks' curly, blonde hair.

"Just when I thought this couldn't get better," Riley said.

I didn't know where to look. Riley and Connor right in front of me, thrusting forward, supporting themselves on their arms. Brooks and Josiah to the side, sucking and licking and groaning. Brooks trailing his tongue down the bottom of Josiah's cock, over his piercings.

And then I was coming again, harder than the first time, my pussy clenching around Riley's cock, drawing an orgasm from him. He in turn, stole one from Connor.

"Fuck... Fuck..." Connor groaned and ground himself against Riley's ass, his fingers digging into his hips. Hard enough that they might leave bruises, but I didn't think either of them would mind. They were laying claim to each other. Cementing a relationship that spanned their entire lives, but was stronger now than ever. No crowbar was big enough to get between them. Or between me and them.

No matter what Connor's father said, we were in this for the long haul.

Josiah was next to come, pulling himself out of Brooks' mouth just in time to spill himself over my stepbrother's cheek and shoulder instead. For a moment, I thought Brooks would be mad, but he looked even more turned on than ever. He almost shoved Connor and Riley out of the way in a hurry to sink balls deep into me. Cum still dripping from him, he slammed into me over and over again before coming loudly and spilling himself into me.

He flopped down over me, then rolled onto his back beside me.

"Are you okay?" Josiah sat down beside me and pushed off his mask.

"Perfect," I said. "You guys always give me the best time." Getting naked with them was top of my list of favourite things to do. Everything else was a distant second and beyond.

He nodded, looking relieved. "I'm going to run the bath for you." Without another word, he slipped out of the room and I heard the water running.

"You need anything else?" Riley took off his own mask. "Tea? Heat packs? The heads of your enemies?" He looked very eager to deliver on that last suggestion. At least, joke about it. I didn't think it was something he'd ever actually act on. Right?

"Have you been reading mafia fiction again?" I teased. Yeah, I'd read that one myself. About the singer who had seven mafia boyfriends, one of which liked to send her presents. He was sweet, in a twisted, fucked up kind of way.

"It's good inspiration." He grinned. "You know there's nothing we wouldn't do for you."

"I do know," I said, tracing a line down his cheek

with my finger. "There's nothing I wouldn't do for any of you either. But I don't need the heads of my enemies." I'd like to think I didn't have any enemies in the first place. What would I do with their heads anyway? They might make interesting sculptures, but that was a bit gory. Not to mention highly illegal.

"Let's get her into the bath," Connor said. "She's going to need cleaning up before we start all over again." When I gave him a look, he pushed off his mask and smiled. "It's Halloween. We're going to trick and treat all night long."

"Especially treat," Riley said. "And eating sweet things like her pussy, and your cock."

"Exactly." Connor nodded. He grabbed my arm and pulled me over to the end of the bed before scooping me up in his arms.

"If you're not careful, I'll forget how to walk," I said.

"When we are finished with you, you won't be able to walk." Connor carried me into the bathroom. Lowering me into the bath was becoming a ritual with us, but I wasn't complaining.

Having four boyfriends was bliss.

25

―――――

LEAH

"Did somebody say party?" Fiona stepped through the open door, into my house. In her hands, she carried a plate of cheese and crackers.

"Looks like the whole gang is here," Whitney said from where she sat on the couch. "There's nothing like a birthday to bring everyone together. Although, the Wilsons' gender reveal was pretty wild."

"I told you, you don't need to make a fuss over me." I shook my head at them. After a beat I added, "Wait, is there something you want to share with the rest of us?"

"Yeah, Whit, out with it," Connor said. He and Riley were in the kitchen, putting the finishing touches on lunch. "Who knocked you up?"

Whitney scoffed. "No one, that's who. I was just making a comparison, smart ass."

He flashed her a quick smirk before turning back to slicing sourdough bread.

"Hey, happy birthday!" Fiona gave me a one-armed hug before placing the plate down on the table.

I hugged her back. "Thank you."

"Can you believe she wasn't going to tell anyone?" Riley asked, shaking a piece of cheese in my direction.

"It's really not a big deal," I muttered. "I'm just another year older, that's all."

"Our woman's birthday is a huge deal," Connor said. "You deserve a bigger party than this." At short notice, they managed Sunday afternoon lunch, leaving Seth and Charlie in charge of a group of snowboarders. Not too many this early in the season.

"I hate to agree with him, but you do," Brooks said. "You've never had a fuss made of you on your birthday." He and I shared a meaningful look. His father and my mother made a fuss of him, but it was always over the top, like he owed them something for remembering the day. I couldn't decide what was worse.

"You deserve it." Josiah put an arm around me and pulled me to his side. "You should be celebrated every day."

"Which reminds me, Brooks and Josiah, you need to tell me when your birthdays are so I can put them in the calendar," Riley said. "Josiah, I bet you'd love a surprise party." He grinned.

Josiah responded with a flat stare. If they tried pulling something like that on him, he'd probably turn and walk back out the door. He was even less inclined to be fussed over than I was.

"No surprise parties," I said firmly. "Unless you're projecting and you want us to throw you one."

"Riley would be ecstatic if you did that," Connor said. "Before you ask, I will fucking stab anyone who gives me a surprise party."

"What will you stab them with?" Riley asked. "Because if you're talking about your cock—"

"With a blunt knife," Connor told him.

"Can we not talk about my brother's cock?" Whitney grimaced. "No surprise parties, we get it."

"Remember that time we threw a surprise party for Francine Davis?" Holly was applying a layer of icing to a cake she brought with her. She'd declared she'd make it herself as soon as she heard it was my birthday. It was a little lopsided, but looked delicious.

Both Fiona and Whitney laughed.

"Oh my God, I'd forgotten about that!" Whitney was almost doubled over. "We were supposed to set up in her house, but her sister forgot to tell her parents about it." She shook her head, laughing too much to continue.

Fiona took over the story. "It was a Thursday afternoon. As it turns out, her parents like to walk around the house naked on a Thursday. So when we let ourselves in, there they were." All three women were laughing so hard, tears poured down their cheeks.

"That, right there, is a good reason not to have surprise parties." Connor waved his knife in their direction. "Sometimes the birthday person isn't the one to get surprised."

That made them howl even harder.

"I think it might have affected their brains," Riley remarked, but he was smiling as much as they were.

"No, Whitney was always like that." Connor moved the sliced bread to a big plate and carried it over to the table. Along with that was a selection of meat, cheese and various other things to make sandwiches with.

"Only since you were born," she quipped. "I was perfectly normal before that."

"The only person who can dispute that suggestion is Josiah," Connor said. He quirked an eyebrow at the older man.

Josiah raised his hands. "Leave me out of this."

"You don't remember kid-Whitney?" Fiona asked.

"Maybe I do, maybe I don't. I'm still not weighing in." Josiah stepped over to the table and pulled out a chair, gesturing for me to sit.

"I think that's wise," Brooks said, sitting on the other side of Josiah. "No good could come out of that."

"None," Josiah agreed.

Everyone took their seats and started to make their own sandwich, and pour themselves wine, or got beer from the fridge.

"I'd like to propose a toast." Riley held up his beer bottle. "To the most beautiful woman in the whole hollow."

"It's so sweet of you to toast me," Whitney deadpanned.

"I meant Leah," Riley said. "You're the equal second-best looking, along with Fiona and Holly."

Whitney regarded him for a moment, then smiled. "Good save, Mr Crane."

"I thought so, Miss Ferguson. Now, where were we?" Riley scrunched his brow. "Right we were saying happy birthday to Leah. Happy birthday, gorgeous."

In unison, everyone said happy birthday, making me blush like crazy.

"Thanks," I muttered, my chin almost to my chest. "Let's eat." If only to deflect from the attention.

Fortunately, that was what everyone did, digging into the fresh ingredients and talking amongst themselves. As for me, I quietly basked in everyone's presence and the fact they'd all turned up for me. Every one of them. I'd known them for a handful of months and they still took the time out of their Sunday to celebrate with me.

Brooks might have anyway; he'd surprised me with a gift of a few books. I hadn't expected anything from anyone else. Which was exactly why I hadn't told them about my birthday. I was worried they'd make a fuss. Okay, part of me was worried they wouldn't. That they'd shrug and no one would care.

The worry was silly, and unfounded, but there it was.

But the reality? I had a feeling, with more notice, they would have thrown a bigger party. Just as well they didn't.

"This is so good," Holly said, groaning around her mouthful. "What's in the sauce you made, Connor?"

He shrugged. "A bit of truffle, some other stuff. Secret recipe."

"It's delicious," I told him. I wasn't disappointed he'd decided not to become a chef, because he loved what he did, but he really was good in the kitchen.

"There's nothing nasty in there is there?" Whitney gave him the side eye, then looking dubiously at her half eaten sandwich.

"What sort of nasty?" Riley asked, barely containing a smile. "Like cum?"

"I was thinking anchovies, but yeah that too." Whitney wrinkled her nose. "He knows how much I hate them."

Connor scoffed. "You can't even taste them. But no, there's none of that in there."

"This time," Riley said ominously. "Beware of future mayonnaise."

Connor pulled off a piece of crust and threw it at him. "Bro, I don't put shit like that in my food."

"Of course you don't, that would mean having to share," Riley said.

"Yeah, let's go with that," Connor said.

Whitney was still giving him a doubtful look, she resumed eating.

"I'm sure he wouldn't put anything gross in there," I assured her.

"Not knowing you're going to eat it," she agreed. "He'd totally do that to me though. One time, he made a cake with salt instead of sugar."

"That was an *accident*," Connor said from behind gritted teeth.

"It was not," she scoffed. "You replaced the sugar with salt and forgot you did it."

He opened his mouth to argue, then shrugged. "It was worth it to see the look on your face."

"You bit into it too," she said with a laugh. "I wish I had a camera to take a photo of the expression on your face. And how fast you spat it out."

"I remember that," Riley said. "That was hilarious. Worst. Cake. Ever. Hey, Holly, there's not salt in the one you made, is there?"

"I guess you'll have to wait and find out," she said looking cagey while forcing back a smile.

Connor broke off another piece of crust, this time throwing it at Holly. "If you put salt in Leah's cake…"

Holly caught the crust and threw it back, hitting him in the side of the head. "Score!"

"What the hell?" He wiped crumbs off his head, while Riley and Brooks struggled not to laugh.

Josiah leaned over and spoke in my ear. "This is why I stay away from people." But he seemed as amused as everyone else, if in a quieter, more reserved way.

"That's very wise," Fiona told him. "I've met people. Some of them are very dubious. Most of them are sitting around this table."

"Including you," Riley told her.

"Especially me." She laughed. "They say you can judge a person by the company they keep. Look at mine." She gestured around the table.

"You must be awesome, because we are," Whitney said. "Right, Holly?"

"Precisely," Holly agreed.

My phone beeped with an incoming text message. I considered ignoring it, but then realised it might be my mother, wishing me a happy birthday. Or maybe one of my city friends.

I picked it up and tapped at the screen, frowning at the preview of the message.

"Shit," I whispered.

"What is it?" Riley was practically shoving Brooks out of the way to take a look.

"The hell, dude?" Brooks pushed him back. "What is it, Leah?"

"The DNA results," I said. I wasn't expecting them

on a weekend, but according to the message they were in my inbox.

"You want to look at them now?" Josiah asked softly, his hand on my shoulder. "We won't mind if you need to step away."

Whatever I needed, they'd understand and be there, even if I asked them all to leave. Which I wouldn't. The last thing I wanted was to be alone right now, with this in front of me.

Before I came to town, I would have done just that. Asked them to leave, or I would have left. Or I wouldn't have told them anything, I would have put the phone back down with the screen facing away. I would have waited until I was alone and dealt with it by myself.

But now I had all of them, my found family, sitting around my table looking at me and worrying that I was okay. If I thought about it too much, I might cry.

I shook my head. "I don't mind if you're here." I realised how that sounded and added, "I mean, I'd appreciate the support." I sat staring at the screen until it went black, then stared for a good few minutes, trying to get up the nerve to open the screen again and open the message.

"It'll be there if you want to look at it later," Whitney said gently.

"I need to know," I whispered. I closed my eyes for another minute or two, then opened them and tapped on the screen. Opened my inbox and looked at the message in black text, contrasting with all the grayed out, already opened messages.

"Here goes." I clicked on the email. Scrolled down and clicked on the attachment.

It opened, displaying a letter with the letterhead of the DNA company on the top. I read the whole thing, once, twice. Trying to comprehend the words. Trying to believe what I was seeing in the results section.

I frowned.

"I don't understand."

26

LEAH

"WHAT IS IT?"

I stared at the screen, vaguely aware of everyone staring at me. Josiah speaking, his hand on my back.

My heart raced. My hands were damp. The churning in my stomach increased. I swallowed back my lunch, but the smell of the ham and salami in front of me was nauseating now rather than appetising.

"Leah. What is it?" Josiah said again. "What do the test results say?"

I tore my eyes from the email. I almost couldn't say the words out loud. If I did, that might make this real. Was there any chance this was a dream? No, my phone felt real in my hand. The email was right there, in front of me, clear as day in black and white.

My ears rang in the silence that was profound as they all stared at me, waiting, concerned.

I swallowed again.

"Negative," I whispered finally. "The results came out negative. I'm not related to Gavin Clarke."

Those were the last words I expected to say. I almost couldn't believe I was hearing them from my own mouth. This was supposed to be the one answer I got that would settle one big question. Science would tell me I was his daughter and somehow we'd figure out the rest of it.

But science gave me nothing but cold words on a bright screen. Negative. Like that wouldn't shatter me right down to my bones. I thought I found myself, but it turned out I was as lost as ever.

"Wait, what?" Fiona was the first to break the shocked silence that followed my words. "You're not?" She reached over to take the phone from my hand and read it for herself. "This doesn't make any sense." She blinked a couple of times, but read the email over again.

"So you're not Coral Clarke?" Holly asked, her lips apart in confusion. "But we all saw the photo."

"Yeah, we did," Whitney said. "It was definitely Leah in that photo." She seemed to be thinking hard, trying to put the pieces of the puzzle together even though most of the pieces were missing. As if somehow it could still match the picture on the box if she kept trying.

"What bullshit is this?" Connor asked. He stared at my phone like it insulted him personally. Or the DNA lab had. If anyone would storm down there and demand an explanation, it would be him, but what would be the point? The results were what they were. He didn't like it, but science had spoken.

I glanced over to Josiah. His tanned face was slightly paler than usual. "I don't know what this means." The last thing I wanted was for people to start pointing fingers at him again just because of this. Whatever was going on here didn't change what happened that day. It didn't change the fact he didn't let a little girl die. If anyone was going to suggest otherwise, they'd have to go through me first. Including anyone in this room.

He gave a barely perceptible shake of his head. "I don't know either. It doesn't change what I saw."

"I know," I said. "It raises more questions."

"Are you going to speak to Gavin?" Fiona placed my phone down on the table.

I considered for a moment before dismissing the idea. As rattled as I was, I had enough sense not to create more trouble for him.

"He's been through enough. Whatever's going on here, my mother might have the answers. I'm going to have to go down and speak to her, face-to-face." She wasn't going to like it, but there was no other way. The only chance I had to resolve this was to ask her in person.

"We'll come with you," Riley said immediately.

"You have work," I reminded him.

"Not if we go tomorrow," Connor said. "We don't have any tours booked for Monday."

"And the pub is closed," Brooks added. "I'm not letting you confront her unless I'm there too."

"Me either," Josiah said softly. "I can get away from the lodge for a while. I'm owed a bunch of sick days."

Whitney leaned forward, her elbows on the table. "You better keep us updated with everything. If I wasn't working tomorrow, I'd be right there with you."

"We will," I assured her. She'd call and text every chance she got if we didn't fill her in regularly. Fiona and Holly too. They'd become almost as invested in this as me. They all had.

"We'll leave first thing," Connor said. He turned to Brooks. "Don't say anything to your dad. I want to see the expression on their faces when Leah asks about all of this."

Brooks rolled his eyes. "No shit, Sherlock. I could have told you that."

"Yeah, well you didn't," Connor said with a shrug. "So I did."

"Are you going to be at each other's throats the entire time?" I asked. "Because I'll leave you behind if you are."

Connor turned his glare on me. "The hell you will. Don't make me tie you up so you can't leave."

Riley grinned. "Can we do that anyway?"

Whitney threw her hands over her eyes. "Can we have this conversation when I'm not here?"

"What are you doing?" Connor asked her. "You know you can still hear us with your hands over your eyes, right?"

"I can pretend." She peeked at us from between her fingers.

Riley chuckled. "I remember that time we were watching a horror movie and you covered your ears, but kept on watching."

Her hands still in front of her face, she flipped him off with both middle fingers. "How old was I? Ten or eleven? It made sense to me then."

"Apparently it still makes sense to you," Fiona teased.

Whitney huffed. "Don't you start." She finally lowered her hands, and picked up her wine to take a gulp. "See, you're all driving me to drink."

"Don't blame us, Whit." Connor took a sip of his own beer.

"I'll absolutely blame you," she said, smirking playfully at him. "If nothing else, it's fun."

Brooks glanced over at me. "I like this."

I offered a faint smile. "Me too." I could tell what he was thinking. We could have been more like them. Always teasing and making fun of each other, but they'd had each other's backs since childhood. Fiona, Holly and Riley too.

Josiah also looked wistful.

"We have each other now," I told them both.

"Yeah, we do," Josiah said. "Whatever happens tomorrow, we've got you." He slipped an arm around my shoulders and pulled me to him until my cheek was pressed against the stubble of his.

"And after tomorrow," Riley added. "We don't care who you are or where you came from. The only thing that matters is who you are right now."

"Did you read that on a motivational meme?" Connor shot him a glance.

"Yes, and I've been saving it up for the right moment," Riley said unapologetically. "Turns out, this is it. You got a problem with that, bro?"

"Not at all, bro." Connor patted his back a little too hard. "It was mushy, but I agree with the sentiment. I don't give a shit about Leah's past, or anyone else's. Right now is what matters." He glanced down at the table for a moment before raising his eyes and nodding at Josiah. His hazel eyes laced with regret.

"Bygones," Josiah said simply.

"Yeah, bygones," Connor agreed.

"Water over the falls," Riley said. "Which is actually ironic. I used to think if we looked hard enough, we might find Coral out there, beside the white water. Or hiding under a tree near the zip line. Or… Whatever. Instead, she found us."

"Yeah, I found you," I said. The rest of it, we had yet to figure out. "It would be ironic though."

"It makes sense to me," Brooks said with a sly smile. "It wouldn't surprise me if Leah was raised by wild animals."

I flipped him off, but laughed at the same time. "Funny, I was going to say the same about you. Except you wouldn't have survived the cold."

His hand went to his chest, right over his heart.

"Direct hit. Damn, woman. That's some aim you have."

"And don't you forget it." I stuck my tongue out at him.

"As if you'd let me." He stuck his tongue out, right back at me.

"As if you want me to," I retorted.

"And you think you missed something not growing up here," Whitney said. "You two are as bad as me and Connor."

"Except you and Connor don't fuck each other," Riley said, grinning at the opportunity she'd handed him.

"Gross, gross, gross," Whitney groaned. "No, we'd never go there!"

Riley just grinned bigger. "You don't know what you're missing."

"Leah," Whitney complained. "Make them stop!"

I laughed. "Riley, stop grossing Whitney out. You wouldn't want to share Connor with her too anyway."

Riley rubbed his chin before pointing a finger at me. "Good point. Sooner or later I'd get involved and that would be like fucking my sister."

"Don't knock it until you've tried it," Brooks said

over the top of his beer bottle, right before he took a sip.

I reached over and poked him in the forearm. "Behave yourself."

He just grinned and took a sip.

"Is anyone ready for birthday cake?" Holly asked.

I realised we'd all finished eating while we were talking and laughing.

"You aren't going to sing happy birthday to me, are you?" I grimaced.

"Of course we are." Riley pushed his chair back and stood to start gathering empty plates. "As loud as we can."

"I have to agree with Riley," Fiona said. "Nice and loud. So the whole town can hear."

"I thought they liked me," I said to Josiah.

"I can kidnap you and take you away from here, if you want," he offered.

"Don't even fucking try," Connor growled, but he clearly knew Josiah wasn't being serious. Unless that was something I wanted. "We're going to sing, and you're going to sing along with the rest of us." He levelled a finger at Josiah.

Josiah gave me an apologetic look and a one-shouldered shrug. "I guess we're doing this." His dark eyes hinted at humour, like he really didn't mind at all.

I made a note of that for when it was his birthday. He'd probably hate being sung to more than I did.

I sighed dramatically. "Fine, I guess I'll have no choice but to let you." But, honestly, it was taking my mind off everything else. For that I was grateful. Too many possibilities were still on the proverbial table. What had my mother done? Who was I really? Did she even have the answers? And if she did, would she give them to me?

Connor looked as if he might smack my ass for suggesting I had any choice, but he helped pack up the table to make room for the cake. Apparently punishment could wait until the other girls had left. He wasn't going to forget, that was for sure.

Holly placed a couple of candles on top of the cake and lit them before putting it in the centre of the table.

As they sung happy birthday to me, it occurred to me that I couldn't even be sure it was my birthday. For all I knew, it could be a completely different date. I might not even be the *age* I thought I was. I could be a couple of years older, or a couple of years younger. I might not even be from Canada.

I managed to smile, but I felt like the cards of my life had been thrown up in the air and scattered on the wind. Did my mother even know?

Was she my mother? If she wasn't, then who was she and what the hell had she done?

27

LEAH

"ARE YOU SURE ABOUT THIS?" Connor glanced over his shoulder to where I sat between Brooks and Josiah. His hands hadn't left the steering wheel. He'd cut the engine, but was ready to start it again at a word from me. He'd drive us all the way back to Aurora Hollow without complaint. Without hesitation.

If I thought ignoring the past and trying to get on with the present and future wouldn't drive me up the wall, I'd seriously consider telling him to take us home. But no, this would hang over me for the rest of my life, always in the back of my mind. That itch I couldn't scratch. Sooner or later I had to do this, it might as well be now.

"I'm sure," I said with as much certainty as I could muster.

Okay, to be honest the certainty was all fake. Deep inside, I was actually terrified. Part of me wished a flare-up would come and give me an excuse to put this off. Yeah, that was silly and I knew it. Who would prefer pain to a confrontation? That list might be longer than I thought, but it wasn't entirely rational. Not in this context anyway.

"Let's do this."

"We're right here with you," Josiah said, giving my hand a squeeze. "None of us is going anywhere. Okay?" He looked me in the eyes, assuring but as nervous as I was. He'd been waiting for these answers as long as I had. A million variations of the truth must have gone through his mind over the years. Finally, we could find out which one was real. After all this time, we could put this behind us.

"You better not," I growled playfully. If any one of them wanted to walk away right now, I wouldn't stop them. If they didn't look back, I wouldn't blame them. But I knew none of them would. They were all in this with me, one way or another.

"Come on then." Connor pulled the key out of the ignition and pushed open the door. As if he'd flipped a switch, we all hurried to get out of his truck and step around onto the front lawn of my mother's house.

Nothing had changed since I was here last. Nothing was out of place. Every last blade of grass was perfectly manicured. They paid good money to have it kept this way. As if somehow they'd cause offence by having slight imperfections outside the front of their house.

The house itself? Grey brick, white windows and a black front door. The place looked like any other house on the street. Nothing about it stood out from the rest.

Of course not. My mother and stepfather wouldn't want to embarrass themselves by being different. My mother was so obsessed with blending in she might have been a chameleon. On the outside at least. Behind closed doors, everything was a different story.

"No wonder you left," Riley said as we approached the front door. "This place looks like suburban Boringville. Let me guess, everyone has two-point-three kids, a dog and a cat."

"How do you have point three of a kid anyway?" Connor asked. He pointed a finger at Riley before the other guy could answer. "I know about mathematical statistics and all that shit. It's a rhetorical question." He narrowed his eyes like he was expecting a smartass remark anyway. Knowing Riley, that was a fair guess.

Riley grinned. "I knew that. What makes you think I was going to take it seriously?"

"I knew you weren't," Connor told him. "I'm trying to circumvent some sort of bullshit response."

"Ask a silly question." Riley shrugged. "Do we do rock, paper, scissors to decide who's going to knock on the door?" He raised his hand, ready to compete for the honour. As if somehow it made a difference who did the knocking. Or the ringing of the doorbell.

Brooks gave him a funny look before stepping past him and pulling a key out of his pocket. He slid it into the front door lock and turned it before pushing the door open.

"Or we could do that." Riley followed him inside. "I should have known you'd have a key. That's kind of our thing, isn't it?" He sounded slightly disappointed, like he'd been hoping for the chance to break the door down.

I hung back, my hand in Josiah's. I hadn't realised it until now, but this wasn't home anymore. The more I thought about it, the more I understood this hadn't been home for a long time. Was it ever? Right now, I felt like a stranger stepping into someone else's house. As if at any moment the police would come and arrest us for trespassing.

"It's okay if you've changed your mind," Josiah said softly. "We can leave." He tucked me to him, his body warm against mine. The smell of pine and leather, reassuring, soothing. Home.

A stark contrast to the smell of cleaning products inside the house. Between that and the buzz of traffic outside. It felt like another planet. So different from the mountains. The air wasn't as cold, but the city was colder in other ways. Impersonal and unwelcoming. A street full of boxes where people lived their anonymous lives. Convenient to amenities, but soulless.

Here, people didn't even know their neighbours' names. Or their business. Or if they were even home. It seemed like such an impersonal way to live.

"Brooks, what are you doing here?" My mother's voice came from the kitchen.

"We thought we'd pay you a visit," he replied.

I gave Josiah a quick glance before sighing and leading him in, letting the door close behind us.

"Who's we..." Felicity caught sight of me as I stepped into the room, Josiah beside me. "Leah, sweetheart! This is unexpected." She stepped over to give me a hug and a kiss on my cheek. Her heels made her taller than me, and her black trousers and white silk blouse made me feel scruffy. Comfortable, but like I hadn't put any thought into my outfit before leaving this morning. Whereas she'd probably been planning this outfit for days.

"Hi, Mom." I gave her an awkward hug back, then introduced her to Connor, Riley and Josiah.

"You're keeping some interesting company," she said, giving them appraising glances as I said their names. Clearly wondering what their relationship with me was. Assuming, correctly, the guys had relationships with each other.

"I don't think I've ever been called interesting before," Riley said.

"I bet you have," Connor told him. "You are interesting."

Riley gave him a sidelong look. "I'm not sure if that's a good thing or not. It sounds like a consolation prize."

Connor jabbed him with his elbow. "It's not a consolation prize. There's nothing wrong with being interesting."

"It's better than annoying as hell." Brooks stepped over to the cabinet where the coffee cups were stored and started to pull some out. He checked the coffee machine before turning it on and starting to heat the water.

"As fascinating as this is," Felicity said slowly, "is there a particular reason for this visit?" She picked up her phone from the countertop and glanced at the screen. "I was just about to head out to drinks with the girls."

"Drinks can wait," I said. "We came to ask a few questions."

She laughed, but the sound was a nervous one. "If it's important, you could have called. I really have to head out—" She took a couple of steps toward the door.

"It is important," I insisted. I didn't come all this way just for her to brush me off and walk away. I knew exactly what she was expecting and hoping for. She'd leave and when she got back, we'd be gone. And any potential controversy along with us. That was how she dealt with problems. By ignoring them and hoping not to be pushed to face them.

But this wasn't going to walk out the door when she wasn't looking. She was going to listen whether she liked it or not.

She exhaled loudly and rolled her eyes toward the ceiling. "Fine." She drew the word out wearily and gestured to the living room. "I suppose we could sit down for a minute or two." As if she was doing me an enormous favour.

Resisting the urge to roll my own eyes, I stepped over and sat, the guys sitting around me.

Felicity lowered herself into a chair and placed her hands on her lap like she was queen of the house. "What is this about?" She looked from me to Brooks and back again, basically ignoring the other guys.

Silence fell for a few long moments while I gathered up the nerve to blurt out what I wanted to say.

"If there's nothing—" Felicity started to stand again.

"Am I Coral Clarke?" I said finally.

She flopped back down, staring at me. Her face was pale, bleached of blood.

"What?" Her voice was shaky. "Of course you're not. Why would you think that?"

In as few words as I could manage, I told her what I knew. At least, what I *thought* I knew. By the time I was done, she looked ready to cry. Of all the responses I expected, that wasn't one of them.

"Who am I?" I kept my voice low, but insistent. I needed her to be honest with me right now. I needed her to tell me the truth once and for all. Then maybe I could start to get on with my life. And Josiah could do the same.

"You're who you've always been," she said, tucking hair behind her ear and patting the rest as if it was out of place. "Why would you go up there? You know how I feel about that place."

Why was this suddenly my fault? I didn't know what I'd find when I went up there. If I had, would I have gone? That was a question I'd never be able to fully answer. I couldn't unlearn what I knew. If I hadn't gone, I wouldn't have met three of my boyfriends. In spite of all the confusion, I would never regret that. Not for a moment.

"That doesn't matter now," I said evenly. "Who am I and what do I have to do with Coral Clarke? I know it's not nothing. If I'm not her, then who am I?"

Felicity rubbed a hand over her forehead. "I can't believe we're having this conversation."

"Why?" I asked. "Did you hope it'd go away? That if you didn't think about it or talk about it, maybe it would all disappear? Somehow I'd never think to ask about the past? Never realise something was going on?"

"I thought we put it behind us," she said, just this side of snappy. "In the past, where it belonged." She sniffed and wiped tears off her cheeks. "You have no idea how hard it's been. All these years, I thought…"

"What did you think?" I hated seeing her like this.

I didn't want to make her cry, I only wanted to understand what was going on. "What happened?"

Did it matter this much? She looked at me like I was breaking a piece of her heart. I could stand up and walk away right now, let her live her life and forget about all of this. Pretend this conversation didn't happen. Pretend I didn't know anything about a missing little girl. Was it so important that I needed to rip my family apart?

But I couldn't walk away now. No one in this room was going to forget. None of us was going to put it aside until we knew exactly what was what. If I didn't insist, then one of the others would. Connor looked like he was just about to jump out of his chair and demand answers. Brooks was almost as impatient. If I didn't insist, one of them would.

I took a long slow breath and sat forward, towards my mother. "Who was Coral Clarke?" I asked gently.

She looked over at me with eyes so much like my own. "There is no Coral Clarke. There never was."

2 8

―――――

LEAH

THE THICKEST SILENCE fell while I tried to process what she said.

"What do you mean there's no Coral Clarke?" Connor was the one who finally spoke. "We have photos of her. And memories of her." He nodded toward Josiah. "Of course she existed."

"She did, and she didn't," Felicity said slowly. "She was a real person, but she was never Coral Clarke."

"You're not making any sense," I said.

She closed her eyes and wiped her cheeks again. "A couple of days after you were born, I made friends with another woman in the hospital." She opened her eyes again. "Her name was Susan Clarke."

"Coral's mother," Josiah said, his voice low. "Gavin's ex-wife."

I nodded and placed my hand over his. "What does Susan Clarke have to do with anything?"

"Susan lost a child," Felicity said. "At least, that was what she told me. I felt sorry for her. Let her hold you." Her voice wavered.

"The day we were supposed to go home, you went missing. One minute you were lying in your little plastic crib. The next minute you were gone. At first, I thought one of the nurses took you to do some sort of check before we were discharged. But then no one knew where you were. You vanished. And Susan was gone too. She told me her name was Jenny. She took you from me."

Her words were met with a stunned silence.

My blood went cold. "She took me to Aurora Hollow."

Felicity drew in a slow, shaky breath through her nose. "It took years to find her and you. She'd told her husband you were his and they planned to raise you. But then the police finally tracked down Jenny. We think someone tipped her off, because she ran right before they found you and returned you to me."

"That's why she was bundled into the back of the car," Josiah whispered. "That's why the police didn't really look for her."

"Because they knew who she really was," Riley

said. "But why did they say she'd run off? Why did they say she was dead?" His brow was heavily creased with confusion.

"Because they didn't want people saying Gavin stole her," Josiah said. "When she left, he broke. No one wanted to think he went along with kidnapping a kid. So they covered it up instead."

"And they blamed you for it." Was it too late to find out who did that and stab them in the eyeball with a toothpick?

"I could have gone along with their lie," he said with his eyes glazed as he thought back. "They were trying to protect Gavin." As if somehow that made everything all right.

"Do you think he knew?" I asked. "Do you think he kept me from my biological family?"

"Gavin adored you," Josiah said. "Maybe he did know and maybe he didn't, but he loved you. He would have done anything for you. Even give you back."

I moved over to sit beside my mother and put an arm around her. "I'm sorry. I know this has dredged up a lot of pain. You must have been beside yourself all those years. Wondering where I was and if people were taking care of me."

She swallowed hard and nodded. "It was pure

hell. You were the first thing I thought about when I woke up in the morning and the last thing at night. When I heard they found you, I was over the moon. But then..."

"But what?" I prompted.

She dropped her head. "You were happy up there. When you came back here, you hated it. You hated *me*. You'd cry and scream and beg to go home. All night long you'd sob and call for your daddy until you finally fell asleep. I felt like... Like there was nothing I could do to make you happy. I even thought about taking you back. But then, I couldn't. You were my baby. I thought if I kept trying, eventually you'd understand. But you didn't. You never wanted to be with me."

"Mom..."

Was she right? I'd always thought she was distant. Could it have been me who was the distant one all along? It couldn't have been easy to bring a kid home when they didn't even remember you. When they only knew one, happy home. It seemed like I hadn't made this easier on her. It wasn't her fault any more than it was mine. It wasn't anyone's fault except for Susan Clarke.

"I don't remember any of it," I whispered.

"You probably put it out of your mind because it

was too traumatic," Brooks said. "This explains a lot, though. I've always thought Leah was a brat." He was holding back a smile.

I smirked at him. "Takes one to know one." I turned back to my mother. "I'm sorry you went through all of that. I'm sure kid-me didn't mean to be difficult."

"Of course you didn't," she assured me. "We could have handled the transition differently. Let you spend time with Gavin while you got to know me. We didn't and that was a mistake. One I can't go back and fix. If I had, I think it would have changed… Everything. But I was so happy to find you again. I insisted that we take you home then and there." Her long sigh was filled with regret.

"Leah has that effect on people," Connor said. "One look and we're hooked." He favoured me with a faint, lopsided smile.

"I don't blame you," I said to my mother. "You did what any mother would have done. You couldn't have assumed Gavin was innocent in all of this. I'm not sure I would have left my kid and hoped for the best."

"Right, he might have skipped town," Brooks said.

"Not a chance," Josiah said. After a moment he added, "But I get it. You didn't know the guy."

Felicity cleared her throat. "What kind of man is he?"

"He's a good man," Josiah said. "He took good care of Coral— Leah. If he knew she wasn't his, he never treated her any different. All he ever wanted was for her to be happy. He adored her and she loved him. He did a good job with her."

Felicity nodded, visibly relieved. She must have wondered all these years what I'd really gone through. Never having a way to know. Only seeing how hard it was for me to adjust to life back here. Brooks must have been a breeze in comparison. Not that I'd tell him that.

"That's what all of us want for Leah," Riley said. "For her to be happy."

"I am happy," I said. "I'm happy in Aurora Hollow. I'm happy now I know the truth."

I'd need to take time to process everything. I'd have to give myself some grace. When I arrived here barely an hour ago, I hadn't expected to hear I'd been kidnapped as a newborn.

Now I knew it, it made a lot of sense. Why I had the feelings and memories I had. Why I appeared in those photographs from school, but wasn't related to Gavin.

"They never found Susan Clarke?" I asked. That

woman had a lot to answer for. She'd disrupted two families and a whole town. So many people. My life. My mother's life. Gavin and Josiah. She left so much pain behind.

"They found her a year or so ago," Felicity said. "Right after she passed away. She'd taken on another identity. They had to do DNA to identify her." She waved a hand vaguely.

"I can't say I feel too bad about it." Her expression was closer to savage delight than it was to regret. That was understandable. She had no reason to have sympathy for the woman who stole her baby.

"I wonder if Gavin knows," I said thoughtfully.

"Doubt it," Riley said. "No one would have told him. It would have brought it all back."

"Is that what it'd do?" I asked thoughtfully. "Maybe he could use some closure as well." After everything, he deserved some peace.

"That leaves one question unanswered," Brooks said thoughtfully. His blue eyes shone with mischief.

I flipped him off.

He grinned unapologetically. "I stand by what I said."

"It's not like we really want to know," Connor said slowly.

"Yes, you do." Brooks was grinning now.

"The asshole is wondering why Susan Clarke took me and not another baby." I sneered at him in a playful, sisterly way. "It's because I was cute."

"Interesting theory," Brooks teased.

"I'll have you know she was the most beautiful baby ever born," my mother said. "That's why Susan took her. And for your information, she's grown up to be a beautiful young woman who I'm very proud of." She gave me a soft smile. "Now the air is clear, maybe we can get to know each other better and make amends for a difficult past."

"I'd like that." I gave her a squeeze. "While we're being nice to each other, I should tell you all of these guys are my boyfriends."

"I figured," she said, to my surprise. "What? I've seen the way they've looked at you since you all walked through the door. And I've seen that expression on Brooks' face since you first met. You two tease each other mercilessly, but you've always cared about each other."

I glanced over at him. "He's all right." I raised my hands in front of my face to block the cushion he snagged off the couch to toss at me. It hit my fingers and fell to the ground with a plop. Right before I snatched it and threw it back at him. He caught it and placed it back.

"You aren't bothered by the fact he's my step-brother?" I asked.

"Would it change anything if I was?" She arched a perfectly shaped eyebrow at me.

I exchanged glances with Brooks. "Probably not," I agreed. "It's a relief to confirm I'm not related to any of them by blood. I'm not, right?" I swung my face back toward my mother.

"Absolutely not," she said, grimacing. "You've been reading too many taboo romance books."

"Is that really possible though?" Riley cocked his head. "I mean, it is taboo romance."

She stared at him for a moment before pushing herself to her feet. "I really should be going. It was lovely to meet all of you."

"Maybe you could come up to Aurora Hollow for Christmas," I said. "We'd love to have you and Lionel."

"I'd like that," she said. "Now everything is out in the open, I'd like to see the place. It was important to you, so it's important to me."

"It's important to me now," I said. "I think you might like it up there. There's something special about the town."

When they weren't treating Josiah like garbage that was. A lot of people owed him an apology for that. I was going to see he got it. They better be good to him or I might start stabbing eyeballs with tooth-picks after all.

She gave me another hug before hurrying out and leaving us alone.

"Well, that was something else," Riley said. "Coral Clarke was really Leah Kent all along. My mind is a bit blown." He rubbed a hand over his head like it was physically uncomfortable.

"Josiah was right the whole time," Connor said softly. "Bro, we should have listened. I'm sorry for being a fucking prick to you."

Josiah rolled his shoulders. "Yeah, well... Bygones."

"If there's anything we can do to make it up to you," Riley said. "Free white water rafting for life."

"I don't need free white water rafting," Josiah said. "Or free zip lining. Or skiing or snowboarding. I can do those things whenever I want." He hesitated for a moment. "There is something you can do, but it's gonna sound dumb."

"Try us," Connor said, gesturing to him with his fingers.

Josiah glanced toward the carpeted floor and started to speak tentatively.

29

CONNOR

"You were what?" Whitney's squeal was almost ear piercing. "Oh my God!"

I shared a glance with Riley and went on handing out beers to everyone. It felt like half the town was here in Leah's tiny rental cottage. She sat on the couch surrounded by her friends, looking over-whelmed.

I was keeping an eye on her. If they got too much, I'd kick everyone out. They were already too much for Josiah, who'd retreated to a corner of the kitchen. I'm not going to lie, I was tempted to do the same. This whole day had been a lot for all of us. I would have preferred my sister and her friends see Leah tomorrow, but it wasn't my call to make. Wild horses wouldn't have kept Whitney away once she knew we returned to town anyway. Nothing would have stopped her from showing up, needing to hear the gossip.

"This is big news for a place like this," Riley said, raising his beer to me in a salute before taking a sip.

"Big news for anywhere," Brooks said. He hadn't taken his eyes off Leah since we got back. At the same time, he'd stayed close to Josiah, as if he couldn't stand to be apart from either of them.

It wasn't until I was taking the top off my beer I realised I'd done the same thing. Watching her, while sticking close to Riley. Drawing comfort from having him close by. Inhaling the scent that was uniquely his and letting it settle my discomfort. Remind me I was home, as long as my found family was around me.

"Yeah, it is," I said with a grunt. "She's handling it." If it was me, I'd probably start to come apart at the seams. I mean, it wasn't every day you got told you were stolen at birth. She'd have every right to be going out of her mind right now. Why wasn't she? Probably because she was strong as fuck. And maybe a little bit because she had us. Multiple shoulders to lean on, to cry on, if she needed them. Support and love. They were everything.

"I don't know what to think." Riley leaned against my shoulder and exhaled.

I snapped my gaze toward him. "What is there to think? She's still the same person. Still our woman. She still belongs here with us." Yeah, I understood what he meant, but I needed to hear the words myself. To remind myself it was true. Leah was still our Leah, no matter what.

"She might not want to stay," Riley said. "Knowing what she knows now, she might think this place is… I don't know, tainted."

I wanted to tell him he was out of his mind, but he was right. Aurora Hollow was the place she was rescued from, in a manner of speaking. The place she'd been brought when she really belonged with her mother. She might decide to pack up tomorrow and go back to the city. Fix the relationship with her mother and forget all about us.

I caught the expression on Brooks' face. He was thinking the same thing I was, while looking between her and Josiah. Clearly torn between the decision to follow her and to stay here with the other guy, and his new life.

"We have to respect her decision," Josiah said, looking as unhappy as the rest of us. "If she wants to leave, we have to let her."

"Fuck." I rubbed a hand over the back of my head. I didn't want her to leave without me either, but I'd spent years building my business with Riley. Walking away from that was going to suck. For a while it would. We could start over in the city if we had to. Right? Maybe we could run jet boat tours around the harbour and out to Howe Sound. Or whale watching tours. Or…something.

Whatever we needed to do, we'd do it.

"We could open that restaurant," Riley said. "You could be the chef and the rest of us could serve the customers." He raised his shoulders and dropped them slowly, obviously not liking his own idea very much.

"We could open a bar," Brooks suggested. "We all have experience doing that now."

Josiah raised his head and frowned at Brooks. "I don't, but I could keep the place from falling apart." It seemed wherever we went, he was in as well.

"We could come up here on the weekends some times," I said. "Whenever we can get away." Yeah, I knew as well as the rest of them a business like that would keep us too busy for vacations in the mountains. If we left, it might be a long time before we returned. Together at least. We might come here separately to visit our families. If I had anything to say to my father. He was going to be pissed if we left. So was Riley's dad. This town was in their blood. In ours. We'd never seriously toyed with the idea of living anywhere else. Didn't want to. We had no good reason to, until now.

"As long as you guys are there, I'm good," Riley said. Always trying to be the chill one amongst us, but not pulling it off today. He didn't want to leave any more than the rest of us. But he also wouldn't give up Leah for anything.

"I'm so glad you know everything now," Fiona was saying. "This is like something out of a movie. I can hardly believe it."

"Me either," Leah said. "But it doesn't really change anything. I'm still just me."

"What, no tell-all memoir?" Holly asked. "I bet it would be an instant bestseller."

"No one would believe it," Leah told her. "Anyway, I don't want that kind of scrutiny. If we can keep this amongst us, that would be perfect." She looked around at each of them.

Whitney made a zipping motion in front of her lips with her fingers. "I won't say a word, but you know this is going to get out, right? Small town and all that. People talk."

Leah sighed. "I know, but I'd like a day or two to

get used to the idea. And some time to talk to Gavin before everyone knows."

"You're not leaving, are you?" Fiona asked, airing the question we'd all been wondering, and leaving the room in a heavy silence. The only sound was the clock on the wall ticking the seconds away while we waited for Leah to respond.

Leah frowned. "Why would I leave?" She looked around at all of us. Saw how expectant we were. "This isn't one of those 'you weren't born here after all, so you have to get out,' things, is it?"

"'Course not," I said before anyone else could speak. "This is one of those 'you might be looking at the place differently,' things. None of us want you to leave." Ironic, considering the first thing I said to her was to tell her to get out of town. Yeah, a guy can change. Even me.

She rubbed her chin and regarded me. "Connor Ferguson, are you actually giving me a choice right now?"

I frowned and straightened up. If that was how she wanted to play it, then I was here for it.

I cleared my throat so I could respond with my best growl. "Fuck no. You're not leaving. If you try, I'm going to tie you to your bed." I nodded decisively.

"Me too." Riley stepped over beside me.

"I think I'll tie you to your bed anyway," Brooks said, pretending to look casual and half-disinterested.

"Me too," Josiah said, speaking quickly during a brief moment of silence.

He was taken aback when Fiona leaped to her feet and hurried over to throw her arms around him.

"We were so wrong about you," she said. "I'm so sorry we were all horrible. What you saw that day must have really messed with your head. And everyone being crappy…"

He awkwardly hugged her back until she stepped away. "Some people would say my head was messed up before that." He seemed grateful for the gesture though. As much as someone could be, while being overwhelmed at the same time. It must have been a long time since he was surrounded by so many people. If it was me, I'd probably be running out the door right now.

I shook my head. "So, it's settled. Leah is staying. Or else." I slid her a smile before gulping down the last of my beer. I might be cocky on the outside, but on the inside I was certain she had one foot out of town. I'd never admit to being scared, not for a moment, but I was almost convinced she was going to start packing, and insist we stay behind. Tell us she didn't love us enough to stay, or take us with her. It was the same fear I used to have with Riley, because we cleared that particular piece of air.

That was another change I needed to make. Stop worrying everyone was looking to hitch the first ride out of town. They weren't. They were all here to stay, and so was I.

"I'm staying," Leah agreed. "You couldn't chase me away."

"I know I couldn't," I said, my smile widening. "I tried. You're a stubborn woman and we love that about you."

"Yes, we do," Riley agreed. "Leah came to town and shook us all up, but it was the best thing that happened to Aurora Hollow in a long time."

"You're so right," Fiona said. "Leah is the best thing to happen to this town."

Brooks cleared his throat but grinned.

I nudged him with my elbow. "You're all right too, sort of. For an asshole." We wouldn't stop giving each other shit. At this point I didn't think anyone wanted us to. We kept them entertained.

"I'm better than all right," Brooks said. "One day you'll admit that."

I snorted loudly. "Keep dreaming, bro." But there

was no heat in my words. Not anymore. I'd save that for anyone who wanted to give Leah or any of the rest of us a hard time. Like my father. When all of this got out, and it would, conversations would take place. If those conversations didn't include being nice to Josiah, I was going to start swinging. The whole town had a lot to make up for when it came to him.

So fucking much.

30

LEAH

"We're right here with you," Riley said as we approached Gavin's small house. "Everything is going to be fine."

"I don't want to upset him," I said. "He's been through enough. What if this pushes him over the edge?" I was more than half-tempted to turn around and walk back to my cottage. The fire was burning inside, keeping the place warm and cosy. Safe. Less… potentially confrontational or damaging.

"If he starts to get anxious, we won't say anything," Fiona said. She'd volunteered to come with us, knowing him better than the rest of us. "We'll keep it to ourselves for now." She gave me a reassuring smile and pushed open the door before stepping inside.

I hesitated before letting my breath mist the air as I sighed, and stamped the snow off my boots to follow her in.

Gavin sat in his usual chair, the TV on, a mug of what looked like hot chocolate in his hands. A marshmallow was floating on the top, melted and gooey.

"Good morning Gavin," Fiona said lightly. "How are you feeling today?"

Gavin took us all in before his gaze settled on me. He huffed.

"Looks like an interrogation squad." He seemed more lucid than I'd seen him before. And more suspicious. Was it too late to walk away after all?

"We're not here to interrogate you," I said gently. I lowered myself to the chair beside his. "We have a couple of questions." I glanced up at Fiona who nodded reassuringly.

"You're her, aren't you?" he asked before I could say anything. "I always wondered if you'd come back."

"I've been here before to help Fiona," I said carefully.

The expression on his face would have given Connor a run for his money. He didn't roll his eyes, but he might as well have. We weren't fooling him for a moment.

"I don't mean the other day," he said. "I mean, you're... Not Coral."

"No, I'm not Coral," I agreed. "I'm Leah."

He nodded slowly, his eyes tired and sad, but still clear.

"You must hate me," he said into his drink. "I didn't know what Susan did. She's dead, you know? Heard the nurse talking about her when she thought I wasn't listening." He paused for a beat before he added, "I thought she cheated."

I frowned. "The nurse? Oh, you mean Susan."

He responded with a rumbling chuckle. "Yeah, Susan. I knew Coral wasn't mine. I thought she'd done the deed with some other man and tried to pass the baby off as mine. Always treated her like she was mine." His eyes were glazed now, but this time thinking back, rather than lost in his own head.

"Yes, you did." Josiah came to sit on the other side of Gavin. "You were good to her. You were good to me too."

"Until I wasn't," Gavin said. "I heard the things they said about you and I didn't know how to tell them the truth. They kept telling me she fell in the river. That was what they wanted me to believe. After a while, I started to think it was what really happened."

He shook his head slowly. "It wasn't until I saw you, Leah, that I knew. I let myself remember. Her mother came and took her back. It was my fault you were kept from her for so long. I think, deep down, I knew what Susan did. I knew and I did nothing to stop it."

I glanced over to Josiah. I wouldn't blame him if he hated Gavin, although Gavin clearly hadn't been in his right mind for so long.

Josiah shook his head slowly. No, he didn't harbour any hatred or resentment. Frustration, yes, but nothing more. No desire for anger or vengeance. He had accepted the situation a long time ago. It couldn't be undone now.

"Am I going to jail?" Gavin asked.

"I think we've all been through enough already," I said slowly. "You said you thought Susan cheated. They can't prove you had anything to do with it."

Honestly, I didn't believe him when he said he knew deep down. If he had, he would have come forward and said something. *Done* something. It was too late to speculate on that now.

Besides, Susan might have run and taken me with her if he'd given her any sign he knew. I could be on the other side of the planet right now.

Or worse.

"I used to hold Coral and wonder what she'd be like as an adult," Gavin said softly. "I knew she'd be beautiful. And smart. I used to sing lullabies to her and tell her she could be anything when she grew up. She… You were always so good at art. You used to sit there for hours and draw and paint. And…make things."

"I still do those things," I said. "Art is my life."

"Coral was my life," he whispered. "I'm glad you came home." He gripped my hand and squeezed, but he seemed to be pulling back inside his own head. "My beautiful Coral. I missed you." He looked confused now, but content at the same time. Like he'd wished, and finally his wish came true.

"I'll visit you a lot more," I said. "If you don't mind me popping in to see you."

"I never mind seeing my baby," he told me. "Why were you gone for so long?"

"I'm here now," I said instead of answering the question. I wasn't sure if he'd understand it anyway. Not right now. If he wasn't lucid, at least he was smiling. I supposed it wouldn't hurt for him to go on thinking I was Coral. It might give him the peace he'd needed for so long.

"She's not leaving town again," Connor said from behind me. "At least, not permanently. We're all her family now."

"Yes, we are," Josiah said. "We won't let anyone take her from us again."

Gavin looked at him sideways. "Good. All of you stay away from the river. It's not safe there." He closed his eyes and seemed to be sleeping.

I eased the cup from his hand and gave it to Fiona. "We'll stay away from the river," I assured him. "We'll let you get some rest."

He mumbled something and nestled down into the seat before starting to snore.

I gave him a long look, smiling to myself. That was the last piece of the puzzle, right in place. The past finally put to rest like it should have been so long ago. I squeezed his hand before I let it go and stood.

"He's life goals," Riley said with a grin. "Falling asleep in a chair like that."

"You do that all the time," Connor told him.

"I do not," Riley protested as we headed out the

door and into the snow. "It's getting heavier. Fuck yeah. We'll be skiing tomorrow!"

"Some of us will be out with the snowplough." Josiah grimaced.

Riley patted him on the shoulder. "I can think of some ploughing we could do for the rest of the afternoon." Grinning, he scooped me up and started off towards my house awkwardly running through the ever-increasing snow.

I squealed in surprise, but let him carry me, my arms around his neck for support.

Connor jogged ahead and was ready with the door open when we got there. Lucky he did, Riley almost tripped and sent us both flying. Somehow we all ended up on the carpet in front of the fireplace, clothes flying this way and that before the door shut behind us.

"Lucky your friend didn't follow us," Brooks said as he pulled off his hoodie and tossed it aside. "She would have had a show."

I laughed. Fiona would have left quietly, possibly shaking her head. She wouldn't have stood there and watched. At least, I didn't think she would. Either way, I put her out of my mind for now, and focused on what was important. My four boyfriends and getting them naked.

"Speaking of watching." Connor pulled his phone out of his pocket and placed it on a table beside the fireplace. Angled so the camera could film all of us.

"What are you doing with all those videos?" I asked him while letting Riley pull off my boots.

Connor shrugged. "Showing Brooks what he was missing. And swapping them for videos of you before we met."

"Now that's a movie night I can get behind," Riley said.

I glanced over at Brooks.

"I haven't shown them to anyone else," he said, raising his hands to either side and smiling like he was innocent as hell.

"You better not," I growled, aiming the threat at him and Connor. "I don't want to see those turn up on the Internet."

"If that happened, I'd kill both of them," Josiah said.

"I'd help him," Riley agreed. He looked straight at the camera and pointed his finger. "And that's a promise."

"I don't share with anyone not in this room," Connor said. He grabbed Riley and pulled him in for a kiss, then kissed me.

In the corner of my eye, I saw Josiah and Brooks

doing the same, their hands wrapped around each other's cocks.

Connor pushed me down onto my back on the soft rug. Riley knelt in front of me and lowered his face between my legs, licking and sucking. He drew my clit between his lips and sucked harder, until I moaned with sheer pleasure.

Connor watched for a minute or two before grabbing lube out of the bedroom and smearing it over Riley's rear hole. Eyes on mine, he readied Riley with his fingers, opening him up before positioning himself and sliding his erection inside slowly.

Brooks and Josiah lay down beside us, Josiah's face close to mine while Brooks wrapped his mouth around Josiah's cock.

"I'm so spoiled," I whispered.

Josiah turned his face and smiled, although the expression was strained as most of his blood was in his lower head. "You could never be spoiled," he assured me. "You deserve to feel good."

"So do you," I said just as decisively. This town had churned us both around and around, but somehow we came out in one piece. That in itself was something of a miracle.

His response to that was, "I love you."

"I love you too," I said. And then I was unable to

form words as Riley pressed a finger inside me, then another. A smile hovering over his lips, he stroked my inside and out, coaxing me closer and closer to the edge.

"Be a good girl and come for me," Riley said breathlessly, his words in rhythm with Connor's thrusts.

I cried out to the ceiling as I came hard, in perfect unison with Josiah. Connor was right behind, thrusting faster into Riley's ass and shouting loud enough to cause an avalanche if he wasn't careful.

"Fuck, fuck…" Connor went still, spilling himself into Riley, his eyes closed, expression of pure bliss on his face. Finally, he flopped forward, catching his breath before sliding out of Riley and rolling to the side.

He was barely clear when Riley knelt between my legs, lined his cock up with my pussy and pushed inside.

"Fucking perfect," Riley whispered.

"She's okay," Brooks teased. He knelt beside me and tapped his cock against my lips.

"Just okay?" I asked, my mouth still closed.

"My stepsister is better than okay, and I'm going to prove it by fucking her mouth." He nodded once. "Now, be a good girl and open up." He tapped his head against my lower lip again until I opened and took him inside.

While Connor and Josiah watched, Brooks and Riley thrust into me, giving me everything they had before they both came, spilling themselves into my pussy and mouth.

I looked at them all, one by one before I slowly, carefully swallowed down every drop.

"Good girl," Riley said with a proud smile. He leaned down to kiss me before sliding out with a contented sigh.

We all lay side-by-side on the rug catching our breath before Connor finally said. "We should be able to see the aurora tonight. If the snow stops in time."

"Hell yeah," Riley said. "We know the best place to see it."

"Can we watch from inside?" Brooks asked. He shrugged when we all turned to stare at him. "It's cold out there."

"Trust us, it'll be worth it," Riley said.

"As long as we're all there together, it'll be worth it," I said. But I was looking forward to seeing the northern lights. I knew it was going to be spectacular. They didn't call the place Aurora Hollow for nothing. Although, there was a certain irony. I was a lot less hollow than I was when I first arrived.

Now, with my four incredible men, and a town I loved, I was finally content.

THANK YOU FOR READING! If you loved this book, please leave a review. For a bonus scene of the guys going on a road trip together, you can download that here.

Ruined

Corrupted

Pucking Dark Hearts

Pucking Hearts Collide

Pucking Forbidden Hearts

Pucking Hardened Hearts

Dusk Bay Demons

Puck Drop

Breakaway

Power Play

Brutal Academy

Book 1 Heartless

Book 2 Cruel

Book 3 Vengeful

Court of Blood and Binding

Book 1 Song of Scent and Magic

Book 2 Crown of Mist and Heat

Book 3 Sword of Balm and Shadow

Book 4 Whisper of Frost and Flame

Dark Masque

Book 1 Bait

Book 2 Prey

Book 3 Trap

Saving Abbie

Book 1 Pitch

Book 2 Pound

Book 3 Session

Book 4 Muse

Book 5 Rhythm

Book 6 Encore

Novella Venomous

Saving Abbie books 1-4

Saving Abbie books 4-6 + Venomous

Ruthless Claws

Book 1 Ivory

Book 2 Crimson

Book 3 Elodie

Harmony's Magic

Book 1 Summoned by Fire

Book 2 Summoned by Fate

Book 3 Summoned by Desire

Shifter's Vault

Book 1 Discarded

Book 2 Deceived

Book 3 Disgraced

My Alien Mates

Book 1 Star Warriors

Book 2 Star Defenders

Book 3 Star Protectors

Academy of Modern Magic

Book 1 Digital Magic

Book 2 Virtual Magic

Book 3 Logical Magic

Complete Collection

Summer's Harem

Book 1: Shimmer

Book 2: Glimmer

Book 3: Flicker

Complete collection

Short reads

Taken by the Snowmen

Jingle All the Way

Also by Maggie Alabaster and Erin Yoshikawa

Caught by the Tide

Book 1–Pursued by Shadows

Book 2 Pursued by Darkness

Book 3 Pursued by Monsters

ABOUT THE AUTHOR

Maggie Alabaster writes reverse harem romance.

She lives in NSW, Australia with one spouse, two daughters, one dog, and countless birds.

Shop direct from Maggie! Store

Sign up for Maggie's newsletter! Sign Up!

Join Maggie's reader group! Join here!

Follow Maggie on Bookbub! Click here to follow me!

Check out Maggie's website- www.maggieal abaster.com